"Is there anything I can do to make it easier?" Julia asked, still feeling guilty after all Linus had done for her.

"If you could relax—" he glanced around as if wary of whatever danger might be lurking about "—it makes it easier to carry you."

"Oh." Julia hadn't thought of that. She wasn't used to being carried and realized she'd been straining ever so slightly as though to keep a small distance between them.

It was foolish, she realized now. Linus had to carry her. The least she could do was try to make the job easier on him.

Reluctantly she pressed her cheek against his shoulder and closed her eyes to the embarrassment she felt. She could feel the surging beat of his heart as he strained to move her uphill as quickly as possible. She let out an anxious breath and focused on breathing in slowly.

Over the scent of the sea, Julia caught a whiff of manly scent—something wild and strong and oddly soothing. She breathed in again, more slowly this time, and felt her fears ebb away.

She was in good hands.

Linus was watching out for her.

Books by Rachelle McCalla

RACHELLE McCALLA

is a mild-mannered housewife, and the toughest she ever has to get is when she's trying to keep her four kids quiet in church. Though she often gets in over her head, as her characters do, and has to find a way out, her adventures have more to do with sorting out the carpool and providing food for the potluck. She's never been arrested, gotten in a fistfight or been shot at. And she'd like to keep it that way! For recipes, fun background notes on the places and characters in this book and more information on forthcoming titles, visit www.rachellemccalla.com.

DEFENDING THE DUCHESS

RACHELLE McCALLA

HARLEQUIN® LOVE INSPIRED® SUSPENSE

Recycling programs
for this product may
not exist in your area.

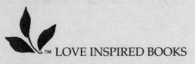 ™ LOVE INSPIRED BOOKS

ISBN-13: 978-0-373-44530-1

DEFENDING THE DUCHESS

www.LoveInspiredBooks.com

Printed in U.S.A.

My God, I trust you. Do not let me be disgraced.
Do not allow my enemies to defeat me.
—*Psalms* 25:1, 2

To my siblings: Nichole, Brian and Brittany.

ONE

Linus Murati stepped into the visual surveillance room of the royal guard headquarters, a three-story brick building located on the Lydian royal palace grounds across the rear courtyard from the garages. "Get me suite 322 on screen, please," he requested.

"I thought you had duchess duty tonight?" Simon accused Linus as he pulled up the view from the surveillance camera.

"I do. Miss Miller has requested an evening in." Linus leaned over the back of his friend's chair and blinked at the image of the white paneled door where he'd left Queen Monica's pretty little sister mere minutes before. "But don't let her catch you calling her 'duchess' just yet. The queen has yet to announce the title—I don't believe Julia knows she's going to be royalty."

"Official or not, that's the name we've assigned to her— wait now." Simon broke off midsentence as the door on the screen opened and the dark-eyed beauty poked her head out, looking both directions before darting down the hall. "Thought you said she was in for the night."

"That's what she told me." Linus watched Julia's progress, switching cameras as needed to keep up with her stealthy excursion down a set of stairs and around a bend in the hall. The woman had changed into shorts and a T-shirt and pulled her thick brown hair into a ponytail. "Do you suppose she's headed to the palace gym?"

"She's going the wrong direction for that."

"Maybe she's lost," Linus nearly growled as the woman took a corridor that led to an outside door. "I told her to page me if she wanted to go anywhere."

"She's out."

The duchess stepped through an exit to the courtyard and skirted a hedgerow, her furtive glances making it clear that she was escaping deliberately—not merely adrift on her way to the gym. "Catch her."

"She won't get through the gates." Linus predicted but ran for the door anyway. The queen's little sister was an American in town on a visit. She wouldn't know her way around the kingdom of Lydia and might get lost if she stepped out alone. Besides that, as the ambush on the royal family just over two months before had taught them, even the most beloved royals could become targets of criminal activity.

Which was precisely why Julia needed a bodyguard.

Linus caught sight of her at the back gate talking to the men in the guardhouse. They wouldn't let her through without a guard. At the very least, they'd check with him before letting her pass.

But as Linus sprinted across the cobblestones, he watched Julia's sweet smile and fluttering eyelashes do their work.

The pedestrian door swung open.

Before Linus could quite recover from his shock, the duchess was through and the door slammed shut behind her.

"What are you doing?" Linus challenged his fellow guards as he bounded up to the open window of the guardhouse.

Galen, a sentinel who'd defied direct orders to save the lives of members of the royal family during the ambush two months before, looked at Linus without chagrin. "She's the queen's sister—"

"I'm assigned to guard her." Linus tugged on the pedestrian door.

Locked.

"Open this door." He glared at Galen, and glanced past him to see that another guard was in the booth. Good. There would still be someone to cover the gate if he took Galen with him. "And come with me."

"Why?" Galen did as instructed and stepped out behind Linus.

"We've got to find her." Linus looked down the limestone street. The duchess had already disappeared. "Did she say where she was going?"

"For a jog."

Linus let out a frustrated breath and wished he'd followed his instinct to set up a chair right outside the duchess's suite. But that had felt too much like he was keeping her imprisoned. It still would have been better than having her lost in a foreign country. The woman could have gone in any direction.

"You go that way." Linus pointed toward the foothills. "I'll head toward the beach." He quickly checked his earpiece to be certain he and Galen could communicate with one another. If they were fast enough, they might catch up to the duchess quickly, but they were already wasting valuable time.

As Galen headed uphill, Linus tore down the streets, slowing at each intersection to be certain Julia hadn't taken a side road. He told himself that she couldn't have gone far. It wasn't as though she'd had *that* much of a head start. He was bound to catch up to her any moment.

But as he passed one side street after another, Linus's fear for Julia's safety grew. What had she been thinking? The sun would be setting soon. He understood that she wasn't used to having bodyguards—she'd already expressed embarrassment over the fuss of organizing the simplest outing—but she clearly didn't appreciate that Lydia wasn't entirely safe.

Sure, the sunset looked peaceful as the gentle waves slapped against the pristine white sand beach, and Lydia's crime rates had traditionally been among the lowest on earth, but that was *before* all the dangers of late. Julia's sister, Monica, had been kidnapped and held hostage just over two months before. And while the man behind those crimes was now dead, that didn't mean the royal family didn't have to take precautions.

Passing the last of the cobbled streets, Linus leaped over the boardwalk and sprinted downhill toward the beach. The sand was riddled with footprints—most of them pointed inland as folks who'd spent the afternoon on the shore returned home for the night. By this hour the beach was nearly deserted.

To his left, the sand gave way to the docks of the Sardis marina. Yachts and sailboats floated peacefully between piers dotted with the occasional human figure, but none of them matched Julia's slender frame. None were jogging.

Linus turned right instead, where the shoreline bent around a jutting bluff, its craggy sides clutching the sandy shore with rutted furrows where children loved to play hide-and-seek. But as the sinking sun gave way to lengthening shadows, the hiding places took on a sinister cast. The duchess could easily disappear behind any of the protruding cliffs. He could pass right by her without even seeing her.

What if she hadn't gone this way at all?

Increasing his pace, Linus raced the sinking sun and tapped the relay button on his earpiece. "Any sign of her?"

"None. You?" Galen panted. His voice carried concern.

"She's not at the main beach. I'm headed toward the bluffs. Let me know if you spot her."

"Should we expand our search?"

Linus checked a chasm between bluffs before answering. No sign of Julia there, either. Should they call for more guards to expand the search? The royal guard had cut loose several men who'd been associated with the former head of the royal guard who'd shot the former king.

They were slowly rebuilding their ranks under the leadership of Jason Selini, the new head of the royal guard. But they couldn't hire just anyone. Royal guardsmen were required to have served four years in the Lydian military. Besides that, after the trouble his predecessor had caused, Jason insisted on carefully vetting all new members of the guard beyond the standard background checks.

Training new recruits took time. Jason had a vision for rebuilding the royal guard stronger than ever, but they weren't there yet. Linus hated to call more men on a case when they were already shorthanded.

And yet, what was that compared to Julia's safety? Linus recalled the stories his grandfather had told him, of *his* days serving in the royal guard. Those men would do anything to protect the royal family. His grandfather's stories had inspired him to become a guard. More than that, he wanted to make his grandfather proud.

He knew what he needed to do.

As he opened his mouth to instruct Galen to call for more guards, Linus cleared the tip of the farthest-protruding crag and caught a clear glimpse of the northward stretch of beach.

A lone female figure ran stalwartly along the sand, her dark brown ponytail bobbing. Though the evening light was almost gone, Linus recognized the bright pink shorts and pale pink T-shirt Julia had been wearing when he'd watched her on the security screen.

For the first time since she'd gone through the palace gate, he exhaled freely. "No need. I've spotted her. She's jogging on the beach. I'll catch up to her. You can meet up with us— we're north of town where the beach access trails connect with Seaview Drive."

"I can be there in five minutes."

"Great." Linus ended the transmission and focused on approaching the duchess without frightening her. Given the darkness and the isolated spot, she'd be startled if he suddenly bounded at her out of nowhere.

He trotted closer until she'd be able to hear him if he called out to her.

"Miss Miller!"

Julia didn't look back. In fact, she appeared to increase her pace. Was she trying to escape him? Maybe she was frightened at hearing a human voice on the isolated stretch of sand.

"Miss Miller!" He was closer to her already. She had to have heard. "Miss Miller!"

Her steps slowed and she turned back toward him, her brown eyes wide, her lips pursed, focused, questioning.

Linus grinned with relief. She'd heard him. He'd get her back to the palace safe and sound. "Miss Miller, please." He slowed down so she wouldn't bolt away again, and called out so she could hear him in spite of the distance and the sound of the waves. "You're not supposed to be out alone."

As he spoke, Julia came to a full stop, watching him. The setting sun cast its golden light across her. She looked positively radiant.

Linus felt his heart give a lurch. He told himself it was because he was glad to have caught up with her. He certainly didn't feel personal attraction toward her. That would be unprofessional. He'd honorably served the royal family for years without ever feeling anything beyond a fervent desire to do his job well.

Granted, the duchess was beautiful. He'd never argue otherwise. But the fast beat of his heart was due only to the exertion of catching up to her, and the fear he'd felt that he might not find her.

It had nothing to do with the way her pursed lips bent upward in a half smile of relieved recognition.

The duchess cast him the briefest look of acknowledgment, lowering her eyes as if feeling chastised for any trouble her escape had caused. Then she turned her head suddenly toward the craggy bluffs just beyond her left arm.

Her eyes widened in shock and her jaw dropped. She started to scream, but long arms reached from the shadows, covering her mouth, scooping her up and carrying her kicking toward the rocks.

Linus snapped into action, hitting the relay on his earpiece as he dashed toward the duchess.

"Galen! Call for backup. The duchess has been attacked." He listened. Nothing. "Repeat—the duchess has been attacked!"

Had Galen heard? Was his lack of acknowledgment due to an overlapping signal delay in his haste to pass the message along to the other guards?

Linus didn't have time to sort it out. Julia's immediate safety was his first priority. He reached the bluffs in time to see the shadowy figure hauling Julia's writhing form up a trail. No doubt about it, the man's actions weren't welcome. Linus wouldn't hesitate to use force against him if necessary.

But on the steep, rocky trail, he'd have to be careful not to risk injury to the duchess. If she fell from this height, she could be gravely injured, even killed.

Julia opened her mouth to scream, but a gloved hand clamped tightly over her lips. She tried to pull away, but hard arms tightened around her. Julia twisted and flailed, trying desperately to free herself from the tight grip of the leather gloves that covered her mouth and lifted her up. She wanted to scream, but she could hardly breathe.

"Don't fight me," the man warned, his arms tightening

as he dragged her from the beach toward the bluffs. "I don't want to have to hurt you. I just need the file."

File? She couldn't make sense of the man's words. What did he mean? Stars danced across her vision. Beyond them, she saw the dark outline of the craggy bluffs that lined the pristine Lydian beach. A deep chasm ran inland, uphill, away from the peaceful coastline. Her captor carried her up and away, out of sight of the guard who was too far away to be of any help to her now.

A fresh shot of terror surged through her. Trails led up the bluffs toward a highway that followed the coastline all the way to the Albanian border. Where was this man taking her? What was he planning to do? The man had come out of nowhere, leaping from the shadows of the rocks and grabbing her the very instant she'd realized he'd appeared.

She had to get free of him before he reached the highway. If he got her in a vehicle, she might never get away.

Her attacker had tight hold of her arms and torso. She tried to jab him with her elbow, to pry her arms free—anything—but his overwhelming size advantage made that impossible. With a desperate lunge, she kicked at him with flailing legs.

Thunk.

Pain shot up her leg as her shin slapped against the protruding rocks of the cliffs.

If she could have, she'd have cried out in pain. Tears stung her eyes, but she refused to give in to self-pity for even a second. The man already had every advantage. She tried again to wriggle free. She couldn't even *see* her captor. How could she fight him?

Suddenly the man cried out and she felt the arms around her slacken.

"Run! To the beach!" The guard's voice echoed across the rocks.

Twisting and writhing, she lunged free from her attacker

as the guard pried him away. Darkness filled the small gorge where the trail cut through the cliffside. Julia lunged back in the direction of the seashore, clutching the rocky sides of the gorge as pain speared up from her injured shin. She half hopped, half dragged herself away, crumbling almost to a crawl as her ankle protested and she scrambled to put distance between herself and the battle being waged behind her.

She looked back to see two shadowy figures fighting in the distance and cringed at the sound of knuckles connecting against bone and flesh. If she could have seen who was who, or even stood on her injured leg, she might have tried to help. Instead it was all she could do to pray silently but earnestly for the safety of the guard who'd come to her aid.

"Who are you?" a harsh male voice demanded. The guard who'd come after her? In spite of the darkness of the evening, she was nearly certain it was Linus. The handsome guard's chivalrous actions the day before—opening doors for her, pulling out her chair, bringing her anything she wanted before she had to ask for it—had left her feeling uncertain of precisely where she stood with him. To her understanding, his gracious behavior was simply part of his job. But at the same time, she wasn't used to it, and had escaped for her evening run alone in part to distance herself from his unfamiliar courtesies.

Now Linus's chivalry had him struggling with her attacker, demanding to know the man's identity and intent.

The masked man didn't answer, but pulled back far enough to throw a punch, sending a stinging blow across her rescuer's face before darting away into the shadows of the craggy cliffs.

Rather than chase after him, Linus spun toward her, the concern on his features only easing slightly when he spotted her.

He ran from the shadows toward her, and for the first time she got a look at his face, certain now of his identity.

Linus. The man had a great smile, but right now his lip was bleeding from his fight with her captor, and his expression was one of concern.

"Are you okay?" He bent down beside her.

Julia pointed up the cliffs. "He's getting away."

"I called for reinforcements. They'll catch him. I can't leave you alone."

Julia had hold of her bloodied shin. Already a bruise was starting to swell above her short socks.

Linus carefully lifted the injured limb. His touch was gentle, his fingers calloused and comforting as he inspected her injury in the waning light.

"I kicked the cliffs while I was fighting to get away." Something halfway between a sob and a laugh came from her lips. "I hurt myself more than I hurt him." Her words were buried under an overwhelming urge to cry. She'd come to Lydia to support her sister, who seemed weighed down by the stress of her new role as queen. How would Monica feel once she found out what had happened?

Julia wondered if she'd been wrong to come to Lydia after all. She'd been unnerved by strange occurrences over the past few weeks. And with her sister in need of a familiar face around the palace, the trip had seemed like a perfect excuse to leave her troubles behind her.

What had happened? Her attack couldn't be related to her troubles back in Seattle. It just couldn't. That would mean whoever had tried to hurt her had followed her halfway around the world.

Nobody was that crazy.

Were they?

The man had said he wanted a file. The request fit too closely with the events back home, and yet...which file did he want? And why? What could possibly be so important?

Linus spoke into his earpiece. He quickly relayed what had

happened, giving his fellow guards their location and instructing them to try to find her attacker among the cliffs, or on Seaview Drive, the highway that followed the Lydian coast.

Then he returned his attention to her. "Can you walk on it?" Linus bent one gentle arm around her torso as if to help her up.

Fighting back tears, Julia realized there wasn't time to cry. What if whoever had attacked her came back before Linus's fellow guards arrived? What if the brute wasn't alone? Were there other men lurking among the bluffs? She shivered as she tried to stand.

With a tentative hand she reached for the guard. His arms were very muscular, the sweat already drying from the breeze off the sea. She placed her hand on his forearm and felt her heart lurch. What did it mean? There wasn't time to consider it. Leaning heavily on Linus, she hoisted herself onto her good foot and tested her injured limb.

"Ow." She winced as her toes touched the sand.

"I need to get you out of here," Linus cautioned her softly. "Can I carry you?"

"You can try." She started to protest that she wasn't as light as she looked, but before she could speak Linus scooped her up, cradling her in his arms as though she didn't weigh a thing. He turned and trotted down the beach, moving as quickly as she had while jogging.

Tears leaked down her cheeks in spite of her efforts to restrain them. Her ankle throbbed. Somewhere in the craggy cliffs behind them, her attacker was probably escaping.

"Do you have a flashlight?" Julia sniffled back her tears.

"Not on me. Sorry."

"Shouldn't we try to find that guy before he gets away?"

"No. We could be outnumbered. That man was a trained fighter."

The sobs she'd been biting back rippled convulsively

through her. Why had a trained fighter attacked her on Lydia's peaceful beach? She slumped against Linus's shoulder, grateful he'd intervened.

"I called my fellow royal guards," Linus assured her, still running. "They'll look for him."

"He'll be long gone."

"Good. Maybe he won't ever come back."

Julia wanted to believe the guard's assessment. The attack had to have been a fluke, a freak coincidence after the incidents back home. The guy was probably some random weirdo. Surely Linus had chased him away for good.

Right? Just some random weirdo who happened to be a trained fighter.

Who'd jumped out of nowhere when she was the only person around, and asked her for a file, mere weeks after someone had broken into the files in her office.

A random coincidence?

Julia heard a low, pain-filled moan and realized it came from her own lips. She'd come to Lydia to support her sister. But what if she'd brought more trouble to the kingdom of Lydia?

Linus paused at a bench. He lowered her onto the seat as he spoke into his earpiece. "I'm returning Miss Miller to the palace."

After another brief exchange, he assured her, "Guards are scouring the bluffs."

"They haven't found the guy who attacked me?"

"They're looking for him." He shook his head apologetically. "It's dark. Those cliffs have a lot of places where a person can hide. Seaview Drive connects to a number of spur roads into the mountains, besides leading to the border. He could be hiding anywhere."

Julia nodded and tried not to let her terror show. Her attacker hadn't been caught after all. He'd gotten away and could return again. Julia shivered, not because of the temperature, but at the thought of her attacker on the loose, somewhere in the vicinity, possibly even watching them from a distance right now. Unable to bear any weight on her bruised ankle, she leaned on Linus and looked past him to the darkness beyond. The sun had set and the first stars twinkled down on them.

The beach looked serene, even in darkness.

But the deceptive darkness hid someone who wanted to hurt her.

TWO

Linus stood panting next to the bench and studied the duchess. A dozen different thoughts warred for attention inside his head, not least among them his concern for Julia's immediate safety. Where had her attacker gone? Had he been acting alone? Between the darkness and the craggy bluffs, the man could be anywhere.

Why had the duchess been attacked? If the man had meant her immediate harm, he could have knocked her off and run away before Linus could have caught up to him. No, it seemed the man wanted to kidnap her or at least drag her out of sight before enacting his plans.

Linus felt his stomach roil with revulsion. He didn't want to imagine what the assailant's plans had been. From what he had observed of her, Julia Miller was a delightful, caring young woman. She hadn't done anything to provoke the attack. Even now, with her face streaked with sand and sweat and her hair ruffled from its ponytail, she looked sweet. Innocent. Pretty.

He put those thoughts out of mind. He shouldn't think about how the duchess looked, and he could grill her on possible theories later. Right now, he needed to focus on her wellbeing. That meant calming her fears and determining whether the injury on her leg warranted a trip to the hospital. And he needed to figure out how to get her off the beach. After chasing her all the way from the palace, fighting off her attacker and then carrying her back through the shifting sand, he was beat. He wasn't sure he could carry her all the way to the hospital, or even to the palace. But he was reluctant to pull any men off the search for her assailant just to fetch them a car.

On top of all that, Linus couldn't shake the question of why the duchess had deliberately run off without him in the first place. Sure, she'd probably underestimated the risk and just wanted a moment to herself. But she could have explained as much to him and he'd have worked something out so that she could have some space and still be safe.

Didn't she trust him?

Or was she running from him?

The thought clamped around his lungs with cold fingers and he stopped panting. During their interactions over the past two days, he'd felt an odd frisson, of attraction or aversion, he couldn't be sure which. But there was something there. He'd told himself not to worry about it, but if it was enough to send the duchess running from the palace without him, then he couldn't ignore it any longer. It would have to be addressed.

Lowering himself onto the other end of the bench, he faced Julia.

In the light of the rising moon, he saw the glimmer of a streak of tears descending down each of her cheeks.

He swallowed. How was he supposed to raise the question that had suddenly become the foremost on his mind? If she really didn't want him around, she certainly wouldn't want to discuss it with him.

"Did I offend you?"

She startled and blinked up at him.

In his exhaustion, his voice had come out a good half octave lower than its usual bass. He probably sounded sinister.

Clearing his throat, he tried again. "I'm sorry. You're supposed to page me if you want to go out."

"When I go out under guard it seems like such a fuss. I thought it would be easier this way." The emotion behind her words strained her voice plaintively.

Linus almost felt guilty for pursuing her. But then, if he hadn't arrived when he did, her attacker would have carried her off. Obviously she wasn't going to share more of her feelings right now, and he needed to get her to a secure location. He switched topics. "How's your leg? Do you need a hospital?"

"It's just a surface injury. I can try walking." She planted her feet on the ground and started to stand, then winced.

Linus scooted across the bench to her side, ready to help in whatever way he could, but unsure if she welcomed further contact with him. It would be easier if he didn't find her so charming, if her predicament didn't bring out every protective instinct inside him, even if he knew where he stood with her.

She rested one hand on his shoulder for just a moment before gulping a breath and letting go, trying again to stand on her own.

A whimper escaped her lips.

"You can lean on me," he offered. They'd lingered too long. He had yet to hear a report of capture, and that wasn't a good thing. They needed to get moving. If Julia's attacker decided to circle around to strike again, he could have easily caught up to them by now, even going out of his way. For all they knew, the man might have accomplices.

"You're exhausted." She met his eyes. Tears still pooled among her lashes.

Linus refused to think about how pretty she looked. "Let me help you. If I need to, I will carry you all the way to the hospital."

Her face puckered and she looked as if she was about to

cry. "You don't need to do that. I can walk." She straightened and forced herself to take a step.

Her injured leg gave way beneath her.

Linus got under her arm in time to prop her up. The woman was too independent for her own good. For her safety, he had to get her off the beach quickly.

Even if it made her cry.

"Come on. Lean on me."

"I hate to be a burden."

"It's that or I carry you." To his relief, she relented to leaning heavily against him, half hopping as they made their way toward the boardwalk that led to the marina. From there, they could connect with the sidewalk along the main boulevard.

They made it a few more steps before the duchess sniffled.

"Are we hurting your leg? We can stop."

"My leg is fine." Her words came out in a strained whisper.

The shock of her attack was taking its toll on her. And her leg wasn't fine—he could feel her shudder in pain with every step she took.

"Please let me carry you again," he requested, unwilling to pluck her up against her will, especially after the way her attacker had manhandled her. He'd only provoke more tears that way. "I'll get you back to your sister."

"No!"

Her sudden insistence surprised him, and he stopped walking long enough to look her full in the face. "Your sister, Queen Monica—"

"Don't tell Monica what happened."

"She'll have to know."

"Please." Julia's grip tightened around his waist, and her free hand clutched his wrist. "She's been through too much lately. She looked so tired today. I don't want her to worry."

"The royal guard was dispatched to look for your attacker. Your leg is injured."

The duchess sucked in a trembling breath. Given his proximity propping her up, Linus felt it ripple through her. She clearly felt strongly about the issue. "*Don't* let on to Monica that anything's happened just yet. There has to be some way around it. I came to Lydia to support her, not to give her more to worry about. We can't put any more stress on her. She already looks so haggard."

Linus saw the queen on a regular basis, and while he wouldn't have chosen the word *haggard* to describe either of the lovely Miller sisters, he had to acknowledge that Queen Monica hadn't been her usual radiant self for the past few weeks. "What's been upsetting her? Her kidnapping was over two months ago. Is it post-traumatic stress?"

"I don't know." Julia let out a long breath. She sounded relieved that Linus was taking her request seriously. "But I've never seen her look this way and it worries me. She's had so many sudden changes—not just the kidnapping and fighting to get her son back—but becoming queen, moving halfway around the world. I thought my visit would give me a chance to help her work through all she's been through, but if she hears what happened tonight it will only make it worse."

The duchess had a point. Linus couldn't deny it. He didn't want to upset the queen further—part of his mission as a member of the royal guard was to protect the royal family, not just physically, but from all harm.

That meant worry and stress, as well. It was the job of the royal guard to worry about safety so that the members of the royal family could focus on their duties without fear. If the queen's haggard appearance came from feeling unsafe, that meant the guards weren't doing their jobs. Linus took that personally.

"Okay," he relented, "I'll see what I can do for tonight at least. Right now we've got to get you back to safety. We've wasted too much time. Can I carry you?" He'd rested enough with all their talking that he figured he could handle the exertion again.

Julia looked up at him with her warm brown eyes, and Linus felt that underlying current he'd sensed before, an emotional charge he couldn't yet identify. Did she suspect that he felt a sense of attraction to her? He had no intention of acting on it, but perhaps she didn't realize that. Or had he offended her in some way? That might explain why she'd run off without a guard.

She still leaned slightly on his arm, unable to put any weight on her injured leg. As Linus adjusted his arm to better support her, he couldn't help but wonder what she was thinking.

The guard had been more than patient with her. Julia realized that. He was also trying his best to be appropriate and respectful, in spite of the circumstances. Instead of hoisting her over his shoulder and trundling her off to the palace, he'd patiently listened to her fears, and even agreed to try not to say anything to Monica yet.

For that, Julia knew she was indebted to him.

On top of that, the man had taken quite a bashing in his fight with her attacker. A trickle of blood leaked from his left eyebrow—that would be a black eye by morning—and his lower lip looked puffy. She examined it in the moonlight perhaps a few seconds too long before she turned her gaze away.

Linus had taken quite a beating on her behalf.

It wouldn't be fair to cause any more trouble. The way he spoke of safety and the need to return her promptly to the palace, she knew he feared what could happen if they lingered near the beach any longer. And in spite of her best efforts, Julia's hobbling was painfully slow. So even though she hated being a burden, Julia agreed to let him carry her again.

He cradled her head against his shoulder as he made his

way uphill from the beach to the palace. It was a steep climb, enough to make anyone feel winded, even if they weren't carrying a cumbersome load.

"Is there anything I can do to make it easier?" Julia asked, still feeling guilty after all Linus had done for her.

"If you could relax," Linus strained, "that would help. When you sit so stiff—" he sucked in two more breaths and glanced around, his dark eyes narrowed as he scanned the storefronts and alleyways "—it makes it harder to carry you."

"Oh." Julia hadn't thought of that. She wasn't used to being carried and realized she'd been straining ever-so-slightly as though to keep a small distance between them.

It was foolish to resist leaning on him. She was only making things more difficult for him. Reluctantly, she pressed her cheek against his shoulder and closed her eyes to the embarrassment she felt. She could feel the surging beat of his heart as he strained to move her uphill as quickly as possible. She let out an anxious breath and focused on breathing in slowly.

Over the scent of the sea and the closed shops and eateries they now passed, Julia caught a whiff of manly scent—something wild and strong and oddly soothing. She breathed in again, more slowly this time and felt her fears ebb away. She was in good hands. Linus was watching out for her. Whatever was going on, whoever had attacked her, Linus and his fellow guards would sort it out. The guards had kept the Lydian royal family safe against awful foes earlier that summer.

They'd see her through this mess, too.

"Almost there," Linus gasped his way up the last ridge to the palace gates.

Glad as she was to be safely back at the palace, Julia felt a distinct swirl of disappointment. Now she'd have to discuss the details of the attack. By rights, she'd have to tell them everything about her fears back home, even if that ended up having nothing to do with tonight's attack. She'd only been practicing law for a couple of years, but that was plenty long enough to understand the problems one could get into from withholding pertinent information.

And she'd have to let go of Linus. She told herself that should be a relief, but as he lowered her to standing, still propped against him to keep the weight off her injured leg while they waited for the pedestrian gate to open, Julia wished she had an excuse to press her cheek to his shoulder again.

Silly. Absurd, really. But it had been so comforting to be close to him.

Linus helped her hop through the door, and a pair of guards hurried over from the guardhouse, quickly forming a human chair with their arms, carrying her sling-style across the lawn.

"To the palace?" one of the guards asked.

"No." Julia started.

"To the guardhouse," Linus explained. "She doesn't want the queen to be worried."

Whatever the other guards thought of her request, they kept their mouths shut and delivered her inside with a minimum of fuss, planting her on a modern sofa in the front waiting area while one of them fetched a first-aid kit. For the first time, Julia was able to get a look at the injury in decent light, and was relieved to find only a nasty scrape and some bruising— painful, but nothing that required a hospital visit.

Linus stood facing the corner, speaking earnestly into his earpiece, scowling. Julia couldn't make out his words, but from what she could see of his face in profile, he didn't look happy.

"They didn't catch him?" she asked when Linus ended the transmission and turned toward her.

He shook his head regretfully.

Julia looked down at her leg. One of the other guards dabbed with gauze at the bleeding parts, cleaning it with gloved hands.

When she looked back up at Linus, she saw the front of his pale blue button-down royal guard shirt rising and falling as he pulled in deep breaths. She sensed his repressed frustration that the shadowy figure had evaded them.

She also guessed that as soon as he caught his breath, he'd want to know everything she could tell him about the man who'd attacked her. If she'd had answers or understood the man's reference to a file, she'd have gladly shared those details. The little bit she knew only made her shiver with greater fear. She wasn't looking forward to reliving those few terrified moments, but worse yet, she didn't want to confess who she feared it might have been.

When Linus looked back at Julia, her attention was focused on Jason Selini, the head of the royal guard, who'd come in from off duty in response to the attack, and now knelt at the duchess's side, bandaging the scrape on her leg.

Linus watched her in puzzlement for a moment, wondering. He hated that she'd been attacked while under his guard. Worse still, he couldn't help wondering why she'd purposely escaped from the palace without him—and if her reasons might be related to her attack.

"Do you need anything?" he asked when she looked up. "A drink? Something to eat?"

"I am a little thirsty."

Linus listed drink options, and Sam, another of the guards, went to fetch them both some juice. With just the three of them in the room, Linus hoped Julia wouldn't feel too overwhelmed. If it had been up to him, they'd be inside the palace and she'd have her sister at her side to comfort her, but Julia had been adamant about not alarming the new queen.

He crouched alongside Jason so that he could look up at the duchess. He didn't need her feeling lectured or looked down upon. "We need to find out everything we can about the man who attacked you this evening." Linus tried to make his low voice less imposing. "What can you tell us about him?"

"I couldn't see him. It was dark."

"You didn't recognize anything about him?"

"Should I have? You fought him. What did you notice?"

Linus swallowed. "He's about six-two, one-eighty. Trained fighter."

Julia shuddered. "Why would a trained fighter attack me?"

Linus watched Julia's face carefully. He'd always been adept at reading people—far more adept than at reading words in books. Now he watched her eyes dart between their faces before she glanced down. She felt ashamed and was weighing her next words.

The door burst open, and more guards poured in.

Julia's eyes widened at the activity.

Linus sensed there was more Julia wanted to say, but she clearly wasn't going to open up in front of so many people. He leaned toward Jason and murmured quietly, "She knows something."

"About her attacker?" Jason whispered back.

The duchess watched the men pour into the room discussing what they'd found on the beach—footprints and sure signs of their scuffle. She looked overwhelmed.

And Linus knew the commotion wouldn't die down anytime soon. The members of the royal guard had always taken their charge to protect the crown very seriously. If possible, they were even more zealous about their duties since the attacks that had threatened the royal family two months before. The attack on Julia was bigger than any threat to the royal family since the crown had been restored with the coronation of King Thaddeus and Queen Monica.

As control central for such events, the royal guard headquarters would be far too distracting a place to hold such a sensitive conversation.

Linus looked back to Jason. "Where can I talk to her?"

Jason looked thoughtful, and Linus could guess what he was thinking. The interrogation room was meant to intimidate, not set a frightened female at ease. In fact, the whole royal guard headquarters was set up for tough men to do hard work. There wasn't a room in the building where the duchess might feel at ease enough to open up about her attacker and the fear that haunted her eyes.

"Take her back to the palace." Jason cleared his throat and addressed the duchess. "I understand you don't want your sister to know about the attack," he conceded. "We don't have to tell her yet this evening. Linus can escort you back to the palace and avoid your sister, but he's going to need to ask you some questions about the attacks. And we'll have to brief the king and queen tomorrow. Will that be okay?"

Julia wrapped her arms around her shoulders as she nodded, blinking back tears. Yes, the events of the evening were catching up to her. Linus feared he might not learn much tonight.

Frustrating. Still, he'd do his best.

"Want to try walking on it?" he asked as Julia placed her feet on the floor and braced herself to stand.

She nodded and eased herself slowly to standing. He felt a moment's triumph at the small victory, but when she tried to shuffle forward a step, she winced.

He swooped in beside her and she took his arm, leaning on him slightly for support.

"I can do it," she whispered.

"You don't have to. We can find a wheelchair—"

"I can do it." Julia grimaced and leaned heavily on his arm as she made her way forward, growing more certain with each step.

Much as Linus appreciated the woman's determination, he wished she'd relent to letting him carry her. It would be so much faster that way, and she wouldn't have to risk straining her injury.

They made it more than halfway across the lawn toward a back entrance to the palace when the duchess stopped to catch her breath.

Linus had been waiting for an opening. He needed to ask her questions. Given the way she insisted on tiring herself out, he feared that once they reached the palace, she'd be too exhausted to talk about the attacks and close the door in his face. Then he'd never learn what doubts had clouded her eyes.

He cleared his throat. "You probably want to forget all about what happened this evening, but before you do that, I need to know everything you were able to observe about your attacker, any clues you might have that would help us identify him."

"I couldn't see him in the darkness. He was wearing a mask."

"I know," Linus acknowledged, thinking quickly. He'd already been briefed about the queen's little sister before he was assigned to guard her, so he knew a few things about her background, and could guess how that might get in her way. "You're a lawyer, right?"

"A trial lawyer."

Having testified in court before about work-related cases, Linus knew about her line of work. "In court, you have to know things with certainty and be convinced of guilt or innocence beyond a shadow of a doubt."

"Yes." She spoke the word slowly as she looked up at him through the misty moonlight. Obviously she had to wonder where he was going with his line of reasoning.

"Right now I need the opposite from you. I know you can't say with any certainty who attacked you, but I want to know your hunches, your gut instincts, your fears. Anything you might have picked up on that would give us a clue about this guy." Linus watched her carefully as he spoke. Even in the moonlight, he could see enough of her face to tell that his own hunch had been correct.

She knew something.

He just had to convince her that it was okay to tell him what it was.

"It's not anything." Julia shook her head dismissively.

Still, Linus felt hopeful. The woman had enough of a grasp on what she knew to discredit it. That meant she could likely put it into words if he could persuade her that it would be acceptable to do so—even if that went directly against her usual practice as a trial lawyer. He waited patiently.

"Back home," she started softly, then pinched her eyes shut. She clearly felt foolish uttering the words out loud.

"Back home?" Linus repeated, prompting her.

"Seattle," she clarified. "Seven thousand miles from here." She huffed a tiny laugh. "Who would be crazy enough to follow me halfway around the world?"

She spoke so softly Linus had to strain to hear her. And yet, as her words sank in, he felt a distinct chill. Had the duchess been threatened even before she left home? If she hadn't been the victim of a random attack, she could be targeted again. Especially if her attacker had already traveled so far to get his hands on her.

"Tell me what you suspect," he prompted softly.

"He said something." She shook her head slightly, but her eyes had met his. "I couldn't have heard him correctly."

"Tell me what you think you heard." He locked on her gaze and held her attention, focusing on imparting a sense of trust, of safety, of acceptance. "The smallest clue can be important," he assured her as doubt rose in her eyes.

She almost smiled then, resignedly, and opened her mouth. Then a small electronic sound cut through the silent night.

"My phone!" Julia pulled back from him and reached for a small zippered pocket on her shorts. "I have a text."

Linus felt his hopes deflate. Whatever Julia had been going to tell him, she wasn't likely to speak up now.

Important as it seemed, his concern about her confession dimmed the moment Julia read the message on her phone.

"Oh, my—" she covered her mouth with one hand, looked up at him with terrified eyes, and whispered past her fingers "—no."

THREE

Did you get what I sent you?

Julia stared at the words, trembling, not just because of the message they implied, but because of the sender.

"What is it?" Linus had been propping her up, and now leaned nearer, the injuries to his face more painful-looking up close.

Julia pinched her eyes shut against the sight.

Linus lifted her hand and read the message on the screen of her phone. "What?" He repeated. "Did you get something?"

"No." She shook her head adamantly. "I didn't get anything. I don't know what it means."

"Julia." Linus spoke softly, his touch soothing as he propped her up. "Talk to me. I saw your reaction. This message frightened you. Why?"

"Did you get what I sent you," she repeated, praying the worlds didn't mean what she feared they meant. "What does that mean?"

"A delivery of some sort? A package?"

"Or a surprise visitor." She didn't want to believe the attack and the message were related, and yet…

"Your attacker?" Linus took the phone from her trembling hand. "Who's the sender? Who is this *Fletcher Pendleton?*"

"It's complicated." Julia tried to straighten out her thoughts. What was the best way to explain?

"Let's get inside." Linus scooped his arm around her waist again, lifting her up to her toes as he guided her toward one of the rear doors of the palace. "Then I need you to tell me."

Emotionally drained, Julia leaned on Linus as he guided her inside, grateful for his steady arm to lean on and his apt understanding of the situation. They needed to get inside before her sister noticed her hobbling across the courtyard and came to check on her. More than that, they needed to sort out what was going on. Had Fletcher sent the thug who'd attacked her on the beach?

She hated to think he'd do such a thing. And yet, given his antics of late, she could almost believe he had.

Linus settled Julia onto a wood-inlaid fainting couch in one of the palace receiving rooms. The cozy parlor was near the rear of the palace and appeared to be seldom used, so they weren't likely to be interrupted. Besides that, it was close to the door, so she didn't have to hobble very far to reach it.

"Are you comfortable? Do you need anything?" The muscular guard, his injuries still untended, looked at her earnestly. Julia couldn't imagine how he could be so concerned about her comfort while his own eyebrow continued to leak blood at a slow trickle.

Linus swiped at his forehead with the back of his hand, his gaze never wavering from her face.

Julia felt a spear of guilt. She wanted to fetch a first-aid kit or at the very least a cube of ice for his swollen lip. The man had done so much to protect her, and now seemed determined to get the sofa pillows arranged around her in the optimum position to ease the pressure on her leg. Were all the royal guards so perfectly sweet and attentive? Julia couldn't recall a time when she'd felt so pampered.

"Now." Linus plunked an ottoman beside the fainting couch and sat, meeting her eyes. "Fletcher Pendleton?"

"He's an engineer. He's brilliant. Probably going to be a millionaire. Or he was." She realized her initial assessment of the man was now grossly out of date.

"How do you know him?"

Julia sighed and thought back in time. It had been one of her first cases as a lawyer. She'd been so eager to do everything right, so earnest, so thorough. In spite of the many cases she'd dealt with since, that one stood out in her mind.

"Fletcher Pendleton created an ultra-efficient engine design for cars. But he was working for a small automotive company at the time, a branch of a successful tech company, Seattle Electronics. Since he was working for Seattle Electronics when he designed the engine for them, they held the patent for his design, but then Motormech Industries tried to buy the design from him."

"They can't do that—not if the company doesn't want to sell." Linus scowled.

Julia was glad the guard understood. "Precisely. I handled the case. It was very straightforward. We settled out of court. Fletcher Pendleton turned over all his design materials to Seattle Electronics. Motormech stepped away from the deal. Seattle Electronics retained ownership of the design and the car went into limited production as the SE323. That was after I was involved. I've only been practicing law for two years, but since then I've been busy with other cases and I didn't pay any attention to what Seattle Electronics was doing."

"What was Seattle Electronics doing?" he asked in a whisper when she fell silent.

"Making cars. But there was a flaw in the design. The SE323 malfunctioned and overheated at high speeds. There were accidents—people were injured, and a couple of Seattle Electronics's employees died testing a car. Seattle Electronics was sued by several different parties." As she stated the simple facts, she looked around at the elegantly decorated parlor, anywhere but at Linus and the injuries he'd received from helping her. His eyes were too kind, his face too ruggedly handsome. She was afraid she might start staring.

"Did you handle any of those cases?"

"No. But since I'd handled the original case, I paid attention whenever I saw their names in the news. Last I heard, Seattle Electronics had filed for bankruptcy protection."

"And Fletcher Pendleton?"

Julia felt an uneasy swirl in her stomach at the mention of the man's name. "That's the strange part. I worked with him briefly when I represented the case. Didn't hear from him for nearly two years after that. Then out of the blue I got an email from him asking if he could meet me somewhere."

"Somewhere?"

"He didn't want to come to the office. He wanted to meet me in private."

Concern swept across Linus's features. "Did you?"

"No. His request struck me wrong. I hardly knew him, and he refused to meet in a public place. He's a rather big guy." Pulled in by Linus's concern, Julia found she couldn't force herself to look away from him any longer. His brown eyes simmered with concern for her safety, reminding her all too clearly of how she'd felt when he'd carried her back along the beach. His strong arms had enveloped her securely, keeping her attacker and her fear at bay.

"How big?"

Julia struggled to think. "Over six feet tall."

"Six-two, one-eighty?" Linus echoed the specs he'd stated earlier.

Julia froze. She stared into Linus's eyes as though she could find the answer there. But all she saw was an earnest desire to help, and determination to uncover the truth.

Linus waited before asking in a patient tone, "Could the engineer have been your attacker?"

Julia hated to impugn a man who might be innocent. And yet, the circumstances all pointed in the same direction. Someone had fought with Linus on the beach. Someone had tried to carry her off. Though she hadn't heard him speaking enough to recognize his voice, neither could she rule him out. Reluctantly she admitted, "It's possible."

"Do you have any other information about him? Contact info?"

"I have his phone numbers, his address, his email address, along with all the emails he ever sent me. I never delete anything—I'm a lawyer. We understand the importance of an evidence trail."

"Good girl." Linus began to smile, but then his eyes narrowed. "*All* the emails? How many did he send you?"

"When I represented Seattle Electronics, he was forthcoming with everything. I got the impression he wanted to cooperate. Maybe he even felt bad for letting negotiations with Motormech go so far."

"Or he wanted you to think he felt bad," Linus surmised.

"Maybe." She sighed regretfully. "Anyway, he sent me a few scattered emails and text messages over the past couple months asking me to meet with him. Not harassing, necessarily, but enough that it creeped me out—that, and his insistence on meeting me in private." It was too much to look at Linus without remembering the feel of his arms around her. She wished she could reach for him and feel his strong shoulder against her cheek again, but she couldn't make such a request after all he'd done for her that evening. So instead she leaned her head back against the pillows and closed her eyes. She felt exhausted by all that had happened and irked by the nagging feeling that she'd forgotten some important detail. But what?

"I'm glad you didn't go," Linus told her, his voice gentle, even caring. "If you get a chance, can you forward me those emails and texts?"

"Sure." She kept her eyes closed, wishing she could block out all memory of what happened on the beach. Rather than trying to remember the details, she wished she could forget.

Linus absorbed the information Julia had given him. He wanted to ask her more questions, but the duchess looked exhausted, and he almost thought she'd fallen asleep. She ought to be tucked securely into her suite before she turned in for the night, but he didn't want to disturb her, not when the fear had finally begun to fade from her features.

For his part, he wouldn't be able to rest any time soon. Not until he'd learned everything he could about this Fletcher Pendleton—including whether he'd recently traveled to Lydia. If the man was currently on Lydian soil, Linus wanted to catch him before he left again.

But then, if the man was after Julia, he probably wouldn't leave the country. Not yet, not until he'd gotten what he'd come for. If anything, he'd try something more aggressive the next time. But what did he want?

Linus didn't understand why the man would be after Julia. Did he resent her involvement in his case, or blame her for the role she'd played in ending the deal he'd nearly made? Perhaps he'd watched her on the televised coverage of Queen Monica's coronation and wedding vow renewal ceremonies. Maybe he thought he could somehow tap into her fifteen minutes of fame.

If Fletcher Pendleton was their man, he already had several advantages over them, including a motive they had yet to understand. Linus was going to have his work cut out for him if he intended to catch Fletcher before the man tried to hurt Julia again. And he feared Pendleton would, indeed, try to hurt Julia again.

Linus took a step toward the door and the floor creaked beneath him.

Julia's eyes snapped open. "Linus?"

He was back at her side in an instant. "Yes?"

"One other thing. It might be important." She made a face. "Yes, it's probably important." She met his eyes and her lower lip trembled.

Linus returned her gaze without wavering and tried to communicate trust, reassurance, safety. She had to feel safe enough to share her fears. At the same time, he wished he could erase the worry that had clouded her features.

"The man who attacked me tonight said something." She pinched her eyes shut.

In spite of his frustration that she hadn't mentioned it earlier, Linus tried to be encouraging. "What did he say?"

"He said—" her voice squeaked as she quoted *"—I don't want to have to hurt you. I just need your file."*

"Your *file?*" Linus repeated.

"I think that's what he said. That's what it sounded like."

"Any idea what he meant by that?"

"I don't know." She paused and wriggled her lips a bit more, clearly fighting back waves of emotions that threatened to leak out with her words. "Well, maybe there is something. It's probably nothing. Even the police seemed skeptical."

"The police?" Linus felt a jolt of alarm snap through him. Though it confirmed his hunch that she'd experienced trouble back home, he still didn't like it. "When were the police involved?"

"Don't tell my sister," Julia insisted. "She doesn't know. I don't want her to worry."

"I don't want her to worry, either," Linus agreed, "but I

need to know what happened. I can't help you if I don't know what's going on."

Julia looked up at the elaborate plasterwork that decorated the high ceiling of the parlor. She appeared to be gathering her thoughts. "Three weeks ago when I arrived at my office on a Monday morning, my office was…disturbed."

"Disturbed?" he prompted when she was silent for some time.

Julia locked eyes with him again. The unshed tears that shimmered behind her lashes begged him to believe her. "I have a violet plant near my window. I was going to water it first thing when I noticed that a couple of leaves had been bent. Violet leaves are very tender. If you bend them they snap and they don't recover—they leave a brown mark right along the bend. Then I looked closer and the dirt was loose."

"Someone knocked your plant over?"

She nodded solemnly. "And then whoever knocked it over set it back up again and put the dirt that had fallen out back under the leaves."

"Cleaning lady?"

"No. The cleaning lady doesn't work weekends, only Tuesday nights, and she doesn't have keys to the offices—she just cleans the restrooms and public areas."

Linus understood. "Too much sensitive client information inside the offices."

"Exactly. After I noticed the plant, I got curious. My office door is always locked—sensitive client information, you know—so no one should have been in there. Nothing else looked out of place. But when I checked my file cabinet, the lock had been picked on one of the drawers."

"How do you know?"

"The lock looked a little scraped up. And when I tugged on the handle, it came open, even though it should have been locked."

Linus tried not to wince at the thought of Julia's hand erasing any fingerprints that might have been on the handle—but then he reminded himself that any criminal fit to pick a lock was probably wearing gloves. Besides, there was a far more important question he needed to ask. "Was anything missing from the file cabinet?"

Her expression clouded immediately. "I scoured it folder by folder. I couldn't find anything missing—not a single page. I called the police and they came to investigate, but I have to admit I felt foolish. They tried to take my case seriously, but other than someone reading confidential client information, I couldn't imagine then what the motive might have been."

"You couldn't imagine it *then*," Linus repeated softly, hoping she'd clarify.

She did. "The file drawer that was damaged contained the *Seattle Electronics vs. Pendleton* file."

He swallowed as the significance sank in. "Where's the file now?"

"In my office back in Seattle."

Linus tried to put the pieces together, but he couldn't make them fit. "The guy on the beach said he wanted your file."

"That's what I *think* he said," Julia said, correcting him.

If the situation hadn't been so critical, Linus might have laughed at her lawyerlike insistence on clarifying that point. But either way, he couldn't see the sense in the man's motive. If Pendleton wanted her file, why would he follow her to Lydia instead of staying in Seattle and taking the file while she was out of the country? Linus shook his head, unable to answer the many questions that were already piling up. Only one thing mattered for the moment, and that was Julia's well-being.

"It's late. I should get you back to your suite."

Julia reached for him without protest, meeting his eyes just long enough to flash him an appreciative smile before turning her attention to her feet. As her small hand settled on his arm and his free arm wrapped around her waist, supporting her as he led her back to the hallway, a new fear hit him.

He liked the duchess.

Not that he'd ever *disliked* her. In fact, he'd held her in complete respect from the moment they'd first been introduced. But it was more than that, now. He'd fought for her. Held her—even held her while she cried.

This was new, dangerous territory, and he couldn't have stumbled into it at a worse time.

Earlier that summer, the head of the royal guard had conspired against the royal family, nearly ousting them from the throne. Linus and his fellow loyal guardsmen had helped the Royal House of Lydia reclaim the throne, and the former head of the guard had died trying to stop them.

Jason had started his term as new head of the guard by thoroughly investigating the records and backgrounds of all the royal guards.

Including Linus.

Jason had discovered Linus's juvenile criminal record, during the rebellious phase he'd put behind him so long ago. Jason understood that Linus wasn't a threat to the crown, that he'd learned his lesson long ago and would never return to a life of petty crime, but the new head of the guard had also made one thing perfectly clear when he'd revealed to Linus what he'd learned.

If Linus ever did anything that would require an investigation, Jason would have to share the details of what he'd learned with the relevant authorities, including the royal family. Linus would most likely lose his job—especially if the revelation was prompted by a strike against him.

The solution was simple. Linus could not allow a single blemish to mar his record in the future, or he might lose everything he'd worked so hard for—his spot on the royal guard, and any shot he ever had at earning his grandfather's respect. His grandpa Murati had bailed him out too many times when he was a teen, and inspired him to turn his life around. Linus wanted to make him proud by being the best royal guard he could be.

Which was why the surge of unfamiliar emotions he felt for Julia were as dangerous as the man he'd fought earlier on the beach. Right now, he was ready to track down anyone who might ever hurt her, to head back to Seattle if necessary to make certain she was safe. But was that the best plan, or were his growing feelings fueling his zeal?

Linus tucked his arm more securely around Julia as they made their way up the stairs to her room. She looked up at him briefly before settling her cheek against the crook of his shoulder.

It was a convenient spot for her to rest her head. It made climbing the stairs easier.

It also sent his heart soaring with emotions he didn't dare explore.

Julia Miller was Queen Monica's little sister, and soon to be a duchess of Lydia. Linus had no right to touch her, except insofar as she needed his help as she did right now. He'd need to get his head on straight and get his emotions under control.

He needed to be the perfect royal guard. Any missteps and he might find himself ousted from the guard. Who would keep Julia safe then?

FOUR

"Paul, isn't it?" Julia greeted the guard who'd been assigned to her the morning after the attack. Of course, she'd known that Linus would be off duty now after working the evening before, but she couldn't suppress the distinct sense of disappointment she felt.

"That's right. And I'm to stick with you wherever you go today, even inside the palace," Paul said apologetically. "Her majesty's orders."

"So Monica knows?"

"She was briefed over breakfast."

Julia nodded, feeling foolish for rising too late to stop her sister from hearing the bad news. But between her late-evening adventures the night before and the fact that she was still used to Seattle time nine hours later than Lydian time, she'd done well to wake up when she had.

"We can still get you breakfast, if you'd like," Paul quickly offered.

"Wonderful." Julia hopped through the open doorway of her suite, still favoring her injured leg.

Paul offered her an arm, which she accepted gratefully. Though the young man seemed perfectly competent and solidly built, Julia couldn't help feeling something was missing.

When they paused at the bottom of the stairs, she studied his face.

"Can I help you?" Paul looked worried.

"Just lead me to my breakfast, please." Julia turned her attention to her feet. She didn't need to look at Paul any longer to realize what was wrong.

He wasn't Linus.

That was it. It wasn't a major flaw. Certainly Paul couldn't help it. But she felt the difference acutely. Though both men wore the same uniform and both were polite and eager to help, Paul wasn't Linus.

Julia tried to think what it was that made the difference. Linus made her feel at ease. Comforted. Protected. Maybe that was all there was to it. Linus had fought off that awful man on the beach.

And yet, she couldn't shake the feeling that there was something more to her feelings than just that.

"Julia!" Queen Monica breezed up behind her as she entered the small dining room, and caught her in a sisterly hug. "What happened last night? I can't believe our guards let you get hurt!"

Julia squeezed back and clarified, "It wasn't their fault. If Linus hadn't caught up to me when he did—"

"Caught up to you?" Monica pulled back just far enough to look into her sister's eyes with confusion. "Wasn't he with you the whole time?"

"Didn't they tell you?" Julia hopped the last two feet to the nearest chair and supported herself by holding on to the back. "I snuck out without a guard."

Monica threw her hands into the air and began questioning her little sister's intelligence just as she had when they were kids.

Julia watched in disbelief. Monica clearly hadn't been informed of that little detail, though from her protests now, she made it clear she knew the rest of the events of the night before.

Linus hadn't told her that Julia had snuck out? Julia felt her heart warm a little more for the thoughtful guard, who'd tried to protect her from her older sister's judgment, even at the risk of drawing blame himself.

"It's okay," Julia rushed to assure her sister. "I'm okay. It's over."

"It's not over." Monica certainly looked upset, which only made Julia feel that much worse. She'd come to Lydia to ease her sister's stress levels, not increase them. "They haven't caught the man who attacked you. All they have is a shoe print."

"Shoe print?" It was the first Julia had heard of it.

"Yes," Paul explained, "they made a cast. Now they're trying to match the sole design to determine what kind of shoe it was."

"They can do that?" Julia was impressed.

"They can try. So far it doesn't match any shoes sold here in Lydia."

Though Paul spoke with a casual air, Julia felt his words like a punch to the stomach. If her attacker's shoes hadn't come from Lydia, then maybe the man hadn't come from Lydia, either. It confirmed her fear that her attacker had followed her all the way from Seattle. She didn't like the implications of that possibility.

Monica squeezed her hand. "I know I said we'd go out today and see the sights, but under the circumstances—"

"I'll stay at the palace," Julia quickly assured her. "There's plenty to see and do right here within the safety of the palace gates." Though she hated missing out on the plans she'd made with her sister, Julia couldn't allow Monica to go out with her. What if something happened? The attack the night before had already upset the new queen enough.

"Thank you." Monica patted her hand, then stood. "I told Peter that we need to come up with some safe activities. I think he's plotting something with his father involving the back lawn and a garden hose. I should check on them."

"I'll catch up to you after I've had some breakfast," Julia promised.

"What are you doing here?" Oliver Janko looked up from the security screen in surprise as Linus came through the door. "Your shift doesn't start for eight hours."

"I've got work to do." Linus slapped down a notebook that held the precious little he'd been able to learn about Fletcher Pendleton from the internet. Other than the pages of search results about the case Julia had represented—which told him little more than she had the night before—Linus hadn't been able to turn up anything helpful about the engineer. "I need to know everything I can about this guy."

Oliver glanced at the pages. "No problem."

Linus smiled. Though Linus was more used to working with Simon, who covered the evening shift, he knew Oliver was just as skilled at accessing information. That was his job. Besides its officers, the royal guard was split between three roles. There were the detectives, like Oliver and Simon, who did investigative work, much of it sitting in front of a computer, though they were trained to work in the field when needed.

Then there were the sentinels—the watchmen who manned the palace gates, patrolled the perimeters any time the royals attended state functions, and rode ahead when the royal motorcade rolled out on official business.

Finally, there were the bodyguards. Linus and his peers were assigned to specific members of the royal household. They'd been shuffled around significantly with the changes that had taken place following the attacks, but that didn't excuse them from knowing their charges well enough to anticipate their needs. Before the recent attacks they had been called upon to rescue the royals from tiring social situations far more often than they were called upon to fight off attackers.

Not that Linus wasn't prepared for both.

"Got a match on that shoe print from last night." Oliver handed him a printout with a picture of the dark cross-trainer and its specs. "Size twelve. Look familiar?"

Linus nodded solemnly as he examined the image and tried to recall what little he'd seen of the man's shoes in the darkness—only a brief impression as the man had kicked toward him. "Looks like what I saw last night. I'll share this with Julia when my shift starts later. How's she doing right now?"

Oliver changed one screen view to a scene of the back yard. The five-year-old son of King Thaddeus and Queen Monica occupied the center of the large palace sandbox, directing his aunt in sand castle construction while he held a hose, filling a moat.

As Linus watched, Prince Peter gestured excitedly with the hose, knocking a section of the castle into a sopping pile of sand. Julia gasped at him, laughing and waggling her shovel playfully at her nephew. The image contained no sound, but Linus could imagine their happy shrieks. With an impish grin, Peter moved the stream of water closer to Julia's toes.

Julia pulled her bare feet away. Though her grin didn't falter, Monica stepped in to redirect her son.

But Linus's attention wasn't on the queen. Julia stood and pulled out her phone, glancing curiously at the screen before answering an incoming call. As Linus watched, her smile fell. Her hand flew to her mouth just as it had the night before when she'd received the text from Fletcher.

Linus leaped toward the door.

Oliver had been briefing him about the shoes as he'd

watched. "Did you hear what I said? The shoes aren't sold in Lydia. It's all on the spec sheet—where are you going?"

"Julia." Linus pointed to the screen, to the clear distress on Julia's face as she spoke on the phone. "Something's wrong."

"Mary?" Julia could hear the frantic tone in her friend's voice, but she could hardly make sense of what the woman was saying. Mary was her sweet elderly neighbor back in Seattle. Julia always kept Mary's cats for her when she was out of town, so Mary had been happy to volunteer to water Julia's houseplants once a week while she was gone.

Now Mary was telling her something about her house—something about a break-in? Julia rushed to clarify.

"Mary? What's wrong? Isn't it the middle of the night over there?"

"Yes, the cats woke me up. That's when I saw the light on inside your house and went to take a look."

"A light on?" Julia was nearly certain she'd turned everything off before she left.

"That's right. I don't know how long it's been on. I wouldn't have noticed it during the day, and I'm not usually up in the night. But the moment I saw it I went to take a look."

Julia didn't like the idea of Mary stepping out alone in the darkness. "Are you there now?"

"I'm back inside my house with the doors locked. I suppose that's silly but it frightened me."

"What did?" Julia felt frightened as well, but she resisted accepting that what her neighbor said was true. Besides that, she didn't want Peter to pick up on her fear, though he was in the midst of a lecture from his mother about the proper uses of a garden hose.

"Your house," Mary moaned. "It's been ransacked."

Julia gasped. "And you went there? Oh, Mary, you could have been in danger!"

"No one's there now—from what I saw I'd guess it happened days ago, maybe even right after you left town. Everything from your freezer was melted in a pile on the floor, and your plants are shriveled up, knocked from their pots. It's a mess. Do you want me to call the police? I almost called them first, but then I thought I should call you."

"I don't know." Unable to guess what the proper response might be without seeing the house herself, Julia looked to where Paul had been sitting just in time to see the guard jump up.

Linus was approaching at a trot across the well-trimmed lawn. What now? Julia listened with increasing distress as Mary recounted all she'd observed before fleeing back to her own house. Books knocked from shelves, cushions torn open, papers strewn everywhere. At the same time, Julia felt a sudden surge of relief seeing Linus, coupled with concern about why he approached her so swiftly. Had something else gone wrong?

"What is it?" he asked in a low voice once he reached her side.

"Just a second, Mary," Julia said then covered the phone, relieved to pause Mary's account of all the things that had been damaged. She met Linus's eyes. "Why are you here?"

"I saw you on the security screen when the call came in. You looked scared. What is it?"

"My neighbor back home," Julia explained quickly. "She says my house has been ransacked. I need to figure out what to do. Should I have her call the police?"

Both Paul and Linus urged her to do so.

Julia returned her attention to Mary, who agreed, and offered to place the call herself. "I'm going to phone them right now. I'll call you back once I've spoken with them."

"Thank you so much, Mary. Stay safe." Julia closed her eyes as she ended the call. From what Mary had told her, the cottage she'd so lovingly decorated must be in chaos. But maybe somewhere in all that mess, whoever had broken in had left behind something that would lead them to the culprit. Was the break-in connected to the attack against her the night before?

It seemed likely. Quite possibly the same person could have committed both crimes. Julia had been in Lydia for two days before the attack. Her house might have been broken into at any time since she'd left for Lydia, the break-in undetected until Mary opened the door. The intruder could have easily found clues at her house that would have told him she'd gone to Lydia. He could have hopped the next flight and arrived in plenty of time to plan his next attack.

But why? What was so important?

Linus spoke, his low voice cutting short the fear that ran rampant through her thoughts. "Do you want to come with me to the royal guard station? I'd like to call the Seattle police as well, but I'll need you with me to fill in the facts."

As she looked up at Linus and met his eyes, Julia felt the reassurance of knowing that she was in good hands. She thanked God for Linus—for his attentive concern and his skill at knowing just what to do. And then she prayed that he *would* know what to do, and that somehow, the attacks would end.

As Linus finished explaining the situation to the police in Seattle, he felt grateful for Julia's confidence in him. He certainly didn't feel confident. First off, the police had pulled up the file on the office break-in Julia had reported weeks before. Based on their notes in that file, they weren't too concerned about what might have happened at her house.

Linus assured them that they needed to be concerned. They agreed to send someone to look at the house and take a statement from Mary.

It was the best he could do from half a world away. He closed the call and looked at Julia apologetically.

"Do you think it's related?" She looked up at him from the office chair where he'd seated her, afraid after seeing her pale face that she might keel over if she got any more bad news.

Linus nodded as he turned his chair to face hers, already analyzing the newest twist in the case. All the things that had happened were like pieces of a puzzle, and this new development felt like an odd piece he'd picked up. He couldn't decide if it fit with the rest or belonged to a different puzzle entirely. Given the proximity to the other events and the previous break-in at Julia's office, he felt nearly certain it had to fit. But how?

Julia scrunched her face in a puzzled expression. "If it was the same person, why would he do so much damage to my house when he was so careful with my office?"

Linus had been wondering the same thing. "Maybe the perpetrator knew you called the police about the office break-in. Maybe he figured you'd notice, no matter how careful he was, so he caused damage instead to throw you off track and hide what he was really after. Maybe he just wanted to scare you."

"What do you think he was after?"

"The file?" Linus raised an eyebrow.

Julia shook her head, perplexed. "What file? The *Seattle Electronics vs. Pendleton* file? They already broke into that file cabinet, but they didn't take the file when they had the chance. Besides, all my work files are at my office. What could they possibly have been looking for at my house?"

"It's hard to guess without seeing what they did to your house."

"Mary tried to describe the damage," Julia said as she sat up straighter, "but I suppose I'm the only one who could tell if something was really missing." She planted her feet on the floor with determination and rose to stand, still favoring her uninjured leg.

Linus stood as well, extending an arm to help her, glad when she placed one hand over his fingers. He had an inkling of what she was thinking, and he didn't like it. "You want to go back to Seattle?"

"How else am I supposed to sort this out? Besides, the break-in could have happened days ago, maybe just after I left town. If it was the same person who attacked me last night, the perpetrator probably followed me to Lydia after they realized I wasn't home. If they're in Lydia right now, Seattle might be the safest place for me." She turned toward the door. "I'm going to see if I can book a seat on the next flight out of Lydia."

Linus mulled her decision as he helped her back through the guardhouse to the palace lawn. Technically, she was a grown woman and free to do whatever she chose. But she was also under his care. He'd been assigned to guard her. How could he do that if she left Lydia?

She was right. Seattle might be safer than Lydia at the moment, but it wasn't the safest place for her, not if the security of her home had already been breached. The safest place for her was at his side.

They no more than made it outside when Queen Monica pounced. "Julia? What happened? Are you okay?"

Julia quickly assured her sister that she was fine, then explained what she'd learned, including her decision to return to Seattle.

"No." Monica shook her head forcefully. "I can't let you go back there. It's too dangerous. Mom and Dad are in Seattle. They can drive over and look at your place."

"I can't let Mom and Dad put themselves in danger," Julia protested. "Besides, this is complicated. Something's going on and I need to figure out what it is. I can't do that from here."

"Julia." A note of warning carried through the queen's voice as Monica took her sister's free arm. "I don't like it. I won't let you go alone."

"There's no way *you're* going to come with me." Julia sounded frightened at the prospect of her sister accompanying her on the journey.

"You're right about that." Monica almost blushed. "I can't leave Lydia right now. But I'll send a guard along with you to keep you safe."

"That's silly. I've already heard that the royal guard is shorthanded after cutting loose the traitors who were part of the attacks against the royal family."

"We can spare one guard to go with you. You've already been assigned a guard, anyway, so it won't short us." Monica looked up at Linus as she spoke. Her smile was half questioning, half conspiratorial.

Linus returned the look. "I'd be happy to go with you, Julia."

The queen beamed at him.

Julia looked back and forth between them. Then she let out a breath that sounded relieved. "Okay then. Linus can come with me. But I *am* going back to Seattle."

Monica grilled her little sister on her plans, then made her promise she'd allow time for lunch with the royal family before she left. With that much decided, Monica returned to the sandbox where the young prince played under Paul's watchful eye. Linus helped Julia up to her room.

"Thank you." She smiled up at him as he helped her down the hall. "Are you sure you should be helping me? Technically I think it's Paul's shift."

"You're right," Linus acknowledged, supporting her again as they made their way down the hall. He wasn't entirely certain why he'd rushed to her side and then stuck there since Mary's phone call had come in—only that Julia had looked distressed, and he couldn't bear seeing her that way without trying to help. "But if I'm going to be traveling with you, I might as well help you now."

"Are you sure you don't mind leaving the country? I'm only buying one-way tickets. I won't know until I get there how soon I can come back."

"I was planning on working anyway. Whether here or there won't matter."

"Your family won't miss you?"

"It's just my grandfather these days, and he's as spry as ever. He'd laugh if I suggested he couldn't stay home without me." He paused as she opened the door to her suite. "If you don't mind, for safety's sake, I'd like to do a quick walk-through."

"By all means. I've got my laptop here—I'm going to look into available flights."

Linus scoped out the sitting room, bedroom and bath, paying special attention to the windows and doorways, but saw nothing that looked as though it had been disturbed. He passed back through the sitting room, where Julia already had flight times up on the screen. "How soon can you be ready to leave?"

"I could be ready to go in under an hour."

She grinned. "Good."

Linus grinned back, feeling eager to head out with her. The sooner they left, the sooner they could sort out what was going on, and the sooner she'd be safe again. And, he had to admit, he wouldn't mind spending time with her, though he'd have to be certain to keep their every interaction above-board. He couldn't give Jason any reason to bring up his long-buried record.

"I can book a flight for 3:00 p.m., then," Julia said, but didn't turn back to her computer.

After staring at her in silence for another moment, Linus

realized he still had the spec sheet on the shoes that Oliver had given to him. If he was going to fit in any more research before their flight, he should ask her now if she recognized anything about the footwear. He pulled out the pages.

"Our investigators matched the shoe print they took on the beach to these shoes in a size twelve." Linus stepped close and unfolded the paper.

Julia sighed as she laid the page flat on the desk beside her laptop. "They sell these shoes everywhere."

"You've seen shoes like this before?"

"Sure. A lot of shoe stores in the malls back home carry them. It's a popular design. He could have bought his shoes anywhere."

"Not in Lydia." Linus watched Julia's face carefully as he revealed the details Oliver had included on the spec sheet. "This company uses sweatshop labor. Lydia strictly prohibits products produced under unjust conditions. These shoes have never been sold in Lydia."

A haunted look entered Julia's eyes. "He could have bought them at the mall near my house." Her words remained level until the final two words, when a squeak of terror penetrated her determined stoicism.

Linus had already suspected her attacker might have followed her from Seattle. But even knowing that ahead of time didn't make it any easier to hear the fear that edged her voice. In fact, he was surprised by the way his heart clenched with concern for her.

But that didn't change the fact that her attacker hadn't bought his shoes in Lydia. Linus made a mental note to ask Oliver to do a specific search on where the shoes were sold. If they could be bought just across the border in Albania or Greece, Linus wouldn't rule out a local. Maybe the text from Fletcher Pendleton was only a coincidence. He couldn't let himself jump to conclusions. But if the shoes were only available in the United States, he'd have to assume trouble had followed Julia from home.

FIVE

As Linus might have guessed, the queen was determined to protect her little sister, and the rest of the royal family rallied around her. By the time Julia emerged from her room, they had a plan in place, beginning with Queen Monica's big announcement.

"We were going to save this news and announce it over dinner on Friday night, but if you leave in the morning you might not be back by Friday," the queen began, love for her little sister shimmering in her eyes.

Julia looked apprehensive.

"Since you are my sister," Monica continued, "and since the Lydian royal family feels you should retain the rights and privileges of an extended member of the royal family, we have decided to grant you a royal title."

"Oh, Monica." Julia's face turned a deep shade of red. "I don't need any rights or privileges—"

The queen cut her off, beaming happily at her sister's red-faced response. "As my sister, the most fitting title you can hold is that of duchess."

"Duchess!" Julia gasped. "I was thinking more along the lines of Her Royal Bookworm."

The rest of the royal family laughed, clearly pleased with

Julia's shocked reaction and relieved to have something happy to share after all Julia had been through.

Linus lingered in the doorway. Even though he'd known ahead of time about the intended title, he still felt a warm glow as the honor was announced. Julia would make a fine duchess.

"I don't deserve—" Julia began.

"Nonsense," her sister cut her off, and the other royals joined in with supportive words.

"I really am honored," Julia assured them when she could get a word in. "But I don't need any privileges."

Princess Isabelle, King Thaddeus's sister, cut her off that time. "You need a bodyguard. That's your right as a titled member of the royal family, and we're going to insist that you have one everywhere you go until the man who attacked you is apprehended."

At the reminder, the room went silent. Julia didn't protest, but looked around the room meekly until she met Linus's eyes. He could see the fear she wanted so much to leave behind. But what frightened him even more was the reluctant gratitude that beamed from her.

He knew how much she hadn't wanted a bodyguard when she'd arrived in Lydia. She'd even gone so far as to sneak out for a jog on the beach to avoid him. If she was glad to have him now, it could only be for one reason.

She knew she was in real danger.

And she trusted him to keep her safe.

Linus swallowed. He'd do everything he could to deserve that trust. But would it be enough?

Julia felt a surge of gratitude as she watched Linus heft her bag along with his. Still unsteady on her injured leg, she'd cringed at the thought of carrying anything. She'd brought only a single carry-on bag for ease of travel, and left her larger suitcase, along with her laptop and anything else she didn't absolutely need, back in her suite at the palace. Still, she knew her carry-on was heavy enough, but Linus insisted on doing anything and everything he could to help her, as long as it didn't require him to leave her sight.

Maybe it was selfish, but she was so grateful for his attitude and conscientious helpfulness. She was glad, too, that her parents had offered to let them stay at their larger home. That way she wouldn't have to be in her own house after dark, and Linus could be nearby, in Monica's childhood bedroom.

While Linus stowed their carry-on bags in the compartment above, Julia settled herself into her seat for the long flight. She'd dismissed her sister's offer to send them via private jet or even first class. Her sister might have plans to make her royalty, but Julia didn't see the need for special treatment.

It wasn't until Linus squeezed his wide shoulders into the narrow seat next to hers that Julia doubted her choice. Maybe *she* fit just fine in coach, but the burly bodyguard could have used a little more legroom for the overnight flight.

"What?"

Julia realized as Linus looked at her in confusion that she had her mouth open in a round O. She snapped her mouth closed, then opened it again. "I think we should try to get you a seat in first class."

"I think they're full."

"Maybe we can make a switch with somebody."

"I'm fine."

"You're squished." Julia had the seat by the window. There were just two seats on that side of the aisle, and Linus still had one foot and most of his arm sticking out into the walkway. "You're going to get hit when the beverage cart comes by."

"I'll pull my arm in then."

"What if you're asleep?"

"I'll sleep with my arm pulled in."

But Julia had already made up her mind. "No, here." She

shifted in her seat until her back was to the window. Then she raised the armrest that had divided the space between them. "You can overflow onto my seat."

"I'm not going to take up any of your seat." As if to prove it, Linus backed farther away, but another passenger passed by and bumped him, so he had to scoot toward her again, but he still didn't seep past the division between their seats.

"You have to avoid being injured so you can protect me."

It wasn't until he gave her a long, slow grin that Julia realized she was fluttering her eyelashes at him. Embarrassed, she put the arm rest back up between them. "Fine, have it your way." She turned to watch out the window and hide the blush that had flown to her cheeks.

There were plenty of reasons why she should not be flirting with her bodyguard. Although technically she wasn't flirting with him, just trying to protect him from bodily injury by beverage cart, but those two were quite nearly the same thing. Anyway, it would be all too easy to flirt with him. He was so good-looking and attentive and polite.

She reminded herself that he was only being attentive because he was paid to watch out for her well-being. And from what she'd seen he was polite to everyone, including a few very grumpy tourists who'd been miffed at him for buying her the last bottle of her favorite flavor of bottled water in one of the airport shops. He'd charmed them both, and she'd gotten to keep her water.

The man was practically perfect, from his white-toothed smile to his deep olive tan, to his broad muscles and kind words. She had yet to find a single fault with him, other than perhaps that she felt like a bit of a helpless weakling every time he rushed to her aid. Linus was a sweet guy. She couldn't risk spoiling their easy camaraderie.

She needed to keep her emotions in check. After all she'd been through, it was no wonder she felt an extra smidgen of attraction toward the handsome guard. But the last thing she wanted to do was make things uncomfortable between them by overstepping the boundaries of their professional relationship.

She'd have to remember to act like she wasn't attracted to him.

Even if she really was.

Linus waited for the duchess to fall asleep before he pulled out his Bible. He needed to read God's word. He needed reassurance and perspective, without the lawyer's sweet smile distracting him.

With a tug on his bookmark, he opened the Bible to the Book of Psalms. He'd been memorizing the Psalms, verse by verse. It was a spiritual discipline that grounded him. With God's word committed to memory, he was never really without a Bible, even when he was in a dangerous situation such as those he'd faced following the ambush two months before.

Those had been frightening days, but God had been with him. Even when he wasn't sure who he could trust—when they'd begun to suspect the head of the royal guard was working against the royal family—Linus had focused on God's promises in the Psalms, and God had seen them through those trials. Jason had replaced the treasonous head guard, and Linus had been promised a promotion.

The only catch was, it had been two months, and other than a jump in his paycheck and a shift in duties as Jason had rearranged the royal guard, Linus didn't have anything to show for his efforts. Though he'd never mentioned it to anyone, he'd have appreciated a new title or even a sentence in the newspaper that he could show to his grandfather—something to let the elderly man know all his prayers over the years hadn't been wasted.

Of course, the whole royal family had been ridiculously

busy since then, and the guards were swamped. There wasn't time for titles or petty news releases. Linus understood. He wasn't complaining.

Still, he felt a tiny emptiness inside whenever he thought of the risks he'd taken, which seemed to have been forgotten already. Reading and memorizing the Psalms would put his problems in perspective. He was up to the twenty-fifth Psalm. As he worked out the words and committed them to memory, repeating them line by line, he heard God's reassuring promises echoing down through the ages.

My God, I trust You. Don't let me be disgraced. Don't allow my enemies to defeat me... Lord, tell me Your ways. Show me how to live. Linus made his way slowly through the Psalm, pinching his eyes shut and repeating the words under his breath until he was certain he had them exactly right. He whispered the words like a heartfelt prayer. *Protect me and save me. I trust You. Don't let me be disgraced.*

Disgraced. The last word made him cringe, and he spoke the plea with sincere pleading, forming his own prayer from the words. *Lord, don't let me be disgraced. Don't let me fail the duchess.* He could imagine the many forms disgrace might take. It was one thing to not have his efforts noticed. It would be another thing entirely if his record of faithful service in the royal guard was marred by a failure to keep Julia safe.

He couldn't let anything happen to her. He'd never forgive himself if he did.

That was part of his role as a royal guard that outsiders didn't seem to fully comprehend. It was more than a job. He felt a mixture of civic pride and honor and devotion that was difficult to explain to someone who didn't feel the same way.

He loved the royal family, every last one of them. Not that he expected them to love him back or anything—it wasn't that kind of love. He and a few of the other guards had discussed it while the royal family was under attack. It was more than the vow they'd taken when they'd become royal guards. They'd risked their lives to restore the crown to the Royal House of Lydia.

And they'd risk their lives again to protect every member of that household.

That included the duchess.

Linus looked over at the sleeping woman who'd pressed herself against the side of the plane to make room for him, and he felt that familiar protective instinct swirling inside him. As he recalled the fear he'd felt when her attacker had struck, Linus strengthened his resolve to keep her safe, and repeated the line from the Psalm on her behalf. *Lord, protect her and save her. Don't let her enemy win.*

Julia had spoken by phone with the Seattle police, who'd already been through her house and identified the intruder's point of entry. Her perpetrator had pried apart the window casings on her three-season porch, which was at the back of the house, out of sight from the street or the neighbors. The intruder had punched through a screen, then knocked out the window between the porch and the main part of the house.

The investigators had also established a time frame for the break-in based on the thawed food that had been tossed from her freezer. The break-in had most likely taken place within the first twenty-four hours after Julia left for Lydia.

Which left plenty of time for the perpetrator to finish tearing apart Julia's house before hopping a plane to Lydia and attacking her on the beach two days after her arrival. If the incidents were related—and she was nearly certain they were—it was entirely possible a single person working alone had been behind everything. It even made sense that the intruder might have spotted the notes she'd left herself as she prepared for her trip and known exactly where to find her.

The police warned her over the phone that, though they'd

completed their analysis of the crime scene, the mess remained. Her job was to note whether anything was missing and let them know.

Julia's hand trembled as she put the key in the front door lock.

When she hesitated to turn the knob, Linus murmured something from behind her.

"What's that?" She turned and met his eyes—anything to put off the dreaded visit, if only for a few more seconds.

"Lord, protect her and save her," he repeated, his tanned cheeks going a bit red. "It's from Psalm 25. I was just praying."

Julia felt a sudden swell of emotion that surged through her throat, carrying tears to her eyes. She turned away before he could see. "Thank you." Her words felt insufficient given his thoughtfulness, praying for her precisely when she needed his prayers the most, but she didn't trust her voice to say any more. Not when she was half a tremble away from reaching for him and burying her head against his shoulder. She knew that such a move would bring her comfort, but it would also vastly complicate their already delicate relationship. It would be all too easy to act on her growing feelings for Linus.

But then what?

Mostly likely, she'd embarrass them both. No, too much of her life was in turmoil to add to the upheaval now.

Instead she turned the doorknob and stepped inside.

Mary's description hadn't done justice to the mess. The pieces of pottery she and her sister had made together years before, which she'd lovingly displayed on the bookshelves on either side of her fireplace, were smashed against the antique tile mantel. Even the tiles had cracks.

And her books! The intruder had ripped out fistfuls of

pages, gutting the cherished volumes. Julia's hand flew over her mouth.

"Are you going to be okay?" Linus asked softly.

Julia nodded, but it took her another few moments to compose herself enough to step farther into the house.

Her furniture was ruined. The upholstery was slashed, the stuffing spilled out. The rugs that covered her oak floors had been tugged aside, but she smoothed one out and found it otherwise unharmed. At least they hadn't stabbed through that.

The kitchen was a disappointment, as well. Every breakable dish lay in shards. The contents of her refrigerator and freezer were strewn about, rotting in rancid puddles. At least her pots and pans had proven durable against the onslaught, though the glass globes of her light fixture were cracked and dangling by the wires.

"Why?" She started to shake as she turned to face Linus. "Why would someone cause so much damage? If they were looking for something, why did they have to break everything?"

"They're just trying to scare you."

"Why? It's like they hate me. Why would someone hate me so much?" She looked at him for a long time, not really expecting an answer. Instead, she found the warmth in his brown eyes comforting, and almost without realizing it, her gaze fell to his strong shoulders. She knew how comforting it would feel to lean on those shoulders again.

And she felt so helpless.

"Do you need to step out?" Linus asked after a moment.

She shook her head, buttressing her resolve to keep her emotional distance from Linus. "I need to look at everything. I'm supposed to determine if anything is missing." She couldn't imagine how she'd do that, not when there was so much destruction to sort through first, and the shock to recover from before she would likely recall any small objects that weren't accounted for.

Probably the perpetrator had planned it that way—to overwhelm her with the destruction and necessary cleanup, so that she wouldn't know what he'd come for until it was too late.

Rather than let that fear paralyze her, Julia took a determined step down the short hallway to the pair of small bedrooms at the rear of the house. The guest bedroom, which doubled as her home office, was relatively stark in its furnishings. The mattress had been turned on its side and punctured, and the bedding was trampled, but otherwise looked undamaged.

Julia took a steadying breath. Maybe the intruder had grown tired by the time he reached the bedrooms. Maybe her bedroom wouldn't be so bad.

She stepped across the hall and flicked on the light, then gasped.

The destruction was worse here than anywhere else. The bedding had been shredded and tossed aside. Her bed was starkly bare, as if to purposely draw attention to the damage. Julia whimpered when she saw it, and stumbled backward to take hold of the doorway so she wouldn't pass out.

Her pillows were riddled with bullet holes.

SIX

Linus stepped toward Julia as her knees wavered beneath her. He'd thought for some time that she looked like she needed a hug, but he didn't feel it was his place to give it, not with the attraction he already felt toward her.

But he couldn't let her fall to the floor. There were too many sharp pieces of her broken belongings littered about. She'd be injured.

He put one arm around her shoulders to support her, and was surprised when she turned to meet him and pressed her face against his shirt.

For an instant he thought he should back away. Maybe she hadn't realized he was moving toward her as she moved toward him.

But she gripped his shirtsleeves and shivered as she fought her reaction to all they'd discovered.

"You've seen it all now," he murmured as he wrapped his arms around her, propping her upright, wishing there was something he could do to make her feel better. She'd already made it clear that she didn't want to lean on him, and yet, her grip on his arms now seemed to be the only thing keeping her on her feet. "Let's step out for a bit, process what we've seen and then come back and look for what might be missing."

Julia trembled against him. At first he wasn't even sure

she'd heard what he'd said, but after a few sniffles, she squeaked, "Good plan."

But she didn't move right away. Linus didn't want to rush her, though he felt she'd recover more quickly if he could get her out of the house. "Is there a place nearby we can go?"

"A coffee shop a few blocks from here. They shouldn't be very busy at this hour."

Linus agreed. It was midafternoon, so they could likely find a quiet corner to themselves. Maybe with a warm drink in her hands and a soothing atmosphere instead of the destruction all around them, Julia could collect herself. Her parents had offered to help clean up the house with them later. It would provide them with an opportunity to note whether anything was missing, though judging from the chaos inside the house, it would take a long time to determine whether things were gone, or simply broken and strewn about.

They darted back to Julia's car, which they'd picked up from the airport's long-term parking. Julia hesitated by the driver's-side door. "I don't know if I can drive right now. Can you—?"

"Sure thing." He took the keys from her. He kept an international driving permit bundled with his passport for trips beyond Lydia's borders so that he'd always be prepared to drive when the need arose.

Julia pointed the way to the coffee shop, and soon they were ensconced in an isolated corner booth with clear view of the door. Linus planted himself in the middle of the semicircular bench seat where he could see anyone who entered the shop. Whoever had attacked Julia on the beach had likely followed her from the palace to the shore, then run along the bluffs or, more likely, driven ahead along Seaview Drive and waited for an opportune moment.

Anyone could be watching them. Linus hoped they'd see he was ready.

Julia scooted into the booth right next to him.

He instinctively moved away from her in order to maintain space between them, but Julia put her hand on his arm. "Don't you want to be able to see the door?"

"Yes, but I don't want to crowd you."

"It's okay." She gave his arm a slight squeeze before letting go and lifting her cappuccino toward her lips. "Your presence is soothing." She lowered her eyes to the surface of her drink as she blew gently on the hot liquid before taking a tentative sip.

It wasn't until she'd swallowed and raised her eyes again that he realized he'd been staring at her lovely mouth for several long seconds.

Their eyes met. She knew he'd been looking at her. She had to know. And yet, she didn't seem to mind. Instead, she held his gaze for a long moment, and he wavered between reaching for her or looking away.

He should look away, talk about something, anything to help him pretend that he didn't want her in his arms again, to camouflage the feelings that he struggled to hide.

He couldn't kiss her. That much was certain. If he got involved with the duchess while she was under his guard, he'd be brought up for review the instant Jason learned of it. His juvenile record would be out in the open, and then what? He could lose his job, lose Julia's respect…he'd lose everything.

Linus realized with shame that he'd slowly begun to lean closer to Julia. She'd started to lean in toward him.

In a moment of insight, Linus realized precisely what he needed to do. If he confessed to Julia about his criminal record, she might lose a little respect for him, but it would also nip in the bud any feelings she might have for him. He wouldn't have to worry about kissing her in a moment of weakness, because she surely wouldn't want a man with a criminal record kissing her. After all, she was a lawyer. She fought to keep the criminals off the streets.

The moment he thought of it, Linus realized it was the right thing to do. Since Julia was adamant about not worrying the queen, Linus knew she'd keep his secret. Working up the courage to speak the words, however, would require a little more willpower.

And timing.

He cleared his throat and sipped his own beverage before glancing at the door. There was a bell above that would jingle if anyone came in. He had yet to hear any jingling. Now might be his best shot, while they were free of interruptions, when he had the bells on the door to give him a split-second warning if anyone entered the coffee shop.

"I'm going to call my folks." Julia sounded suddenly self-conscious as she pulled out her phone before he could speak. She called and updated her parents on what she'd found, then made plans to meet them back at the house later to go through things.

While she launched into what promised to be a long conversation, Linus sipped his drink and prayed silently about what to do next. Item one on his list was to not kiss the duchess. Preferably to not even touch her, if he could avoid it.

No, there were plenty far more pressing things he ought to be thinking about. Until Julia was safe, he'd be at her side. After all, as Jason had stressed to him earlier, Linus was the only guard who'd seen Julia's attacker. He'd fought with him, observed things, maybe even learned enough about the man from fighting him to recognize him again if he had the chance, in spite of the darkness and his mask. Linus needed to be Julia's guard until they caught her attacker.

If he wanted to escape from the temptation she presented, he needed to solve this case.

But what should they focus on next? He didn't see much

point in discussing the mess at the house. Not now. That would only traumatize Julia further, and they could discuss it at length when they met her parents there later.

He pulled out his phone and checked his emails, grateful to see that Oliver had passed his notes on Fletcher Pendleton on to Simon, and the guard had dug up a little information. By the time he'd finished reading, Julia had ended her call with her parents.

"We're meeting them at the house at four?" He stated the time he'd heard her note, two hours away.

"Yes. My mom has a meeting until shortly before then. She and my dad are going to round up some cleaning supplies for us."

To Linus's relief, Julia spoke calmly.

He hated to bring up anything that might distress her, but he needed to go over the facts Simon had forwarded him about his research on Fletcher Pendleton and Seattle Electronics.

After another sip of her cappuccino, Julia smiled at him calmly. "What about you? I saw you checking your messages. Learn anything?"

"The guards have forwarded me everything they've managed to dig up on Pendleton."

"Oh?" She clearly wanted to sound casual, but fear rippled through that lone syllable.

"There's not much out there, other than the articles about the case with Seattle Electronics, but those don't tell us anything more than what we already knew. Pendleton keeps a low profile. No social networking profiles, no court records. He wasn't listed among the arrivals at the Lydian airport on any flights since you arrived in the country, but that's inconclusive."

"He could have flown to a neighboring country and rented a car to drive the rest of the way. Or he could have traveled under another name."

"But he wasn't on our flight out of Lydia, and the next flight to the U.S. is still in the air. So if we want to test my theory, we need to act quickly."

"What's your theory?" A note of hope entered Julia's voice.

"Let's call him. Say you've given his request some thought."

Julia's eyes widened. "That would be the quickest way to find out if he's in Seattle. Do you think I should actually meet with him?"

"We'll see. Certainly not alone. I'm not going to put you at risk, but if Pendleton is our man, we need to find out where he's been and where he is now, who he's working with and what he's after. We can try to learn as much as we can over the phone, like what the text he sent you is supposed to mean. If he wants to meet, let's pick a spot ahead of time. Tell him you'll have a friend with you. We can approach slowly from a distance, and if you don't feel safe, we can leave."

Julia nodded slowly. "We should be able to tell if he was the man who attacked me. He should have bruises. You saw his eyes."

"I think I could recognize his eyes—at least to some degree. And we have the shoe print from the beach. Size twelve. I'm an eleven-and-a-half, so that's slightly bigger than my foot." He watched her face carefully as he asked, "Do you feel comfortable doing this? I don't want to ask you to do any—"

"I want to do it." She cut him off with authority in her voice. "I want to catch this guy and end this. I went to Lydia to support my sister, and until this situation is laid to rest, she's only going to worry that much more. Besides—" she gave him a soft smile "—you said yourself, he wasn't on our plane. I'd have recognized him. And the next flight is in the air. We need to act quickly if we don't want to lose the advantage of knowing whether he may have been in Lydia. Now, let's pick that location if he still wants to meet."

Since Linus didn't know Seattle, he let Julia propose a spot—plenty far from the airport so Pendleton couldn't hop off a flight and pop over to meet with them. She picked a public park only a few blocks from the address she had listed for him, so he was sure to know the place. Then she pulled out her phone with trembling hands.

Her fingers hovered motionless above the phone. "What was that prayer you prayed earlier?"

"Lord, protect her and save her." He recited the heartfelt words from memory.

"Can you keep praying while I place the call?" The tiniest edge of fear entered her voice.

"I'd be glad to."

While Linus prayed the words silently, he listened with half an ear to Julia's side of the call. To his relief, she spoke with an even voice, and he heard her make plans to meet later that evening at the park they'd selected.

When she asked the engineer about the text, Linus felt proud that she managed to keep her voice steady.

"A package?" Julia repeated. "You sent it to Lydia? I'll ask, but I haven't seen anything. What kind of package?"

Linus couldn't hear the answer. The conversation ended shortly thereafter. Julia let out a shaking breath and met his eyes as she put away her phone. "He wants to meet at eight."

Linus had heard as much. "The next connecting flight from Lydia is scheduled to arrive in Seattle at six fifteen."

"If he's on that flight, he could make it." The wavering note in her voice revealed uncertainty and disappointment. "He said he was busy until then. I suppose he could have answered his phone on the plane if they're over land by now, and near a tower."

"I suppose." Linus let out a long breath. He knew phones weren't supposed to be in use during flights, but if Pendleton was behind the attacks, Linus couldn't expect the man to follow rules about phone use. Or he could have hopped an earlier flight or skipped the border and flown back to Seattle from Albania or Greece. They couldn't rule out whether Fletcher Pendleton had personally attacked Julia in Lydia.

Not yet, anyway.

"What did he tell you about the package?"

Julia made a bewildered face. "He said he sent something to me in Lydia. I asked him what kind of package, but he told me he'd explain when we meet tonight."

"A package." Linus nodded. "Right." He still wasn't convinced Fletcher wasn't referring to the attack on the beach, but they'd have a chance to grill the man soon enough.

They still had almost two hours before they'd arranged to meet Julia's parents at her house. He didn't see any point in returning to the site until then—especially not given Julia's current distress. But he had another place he wanted to see.

Julia drained the last of her cappuccino. "What should we do now?"

"I'd like to see your office."

She offered him a tiny smile. "You want to check the broken leaves on my violet plant for clues?"

He smiled back, pleased she was making an effort to retain her sense of humor, though he sensed it strained her to do so. "And the drawer on your file cabinet. I know you already looked, but I want to see those files."

"Sounds like as good a plan as any. Let's go." She scooted out of the booth.

Linus followed, still praying silently—that God would protect Julia, and that God would give him wisdom. He didn't know too much about legal documents, but he felt certain there had to be a connection between the break-in at Julia's office and her attacker's request for a file. And maybe, while they were at it, he could find a way to break the news to her that he wasn't the man she thought him to be. His grandfather had always said honesty was the best policy. And if it helped him keep his distance from the lovely duchess, all the better.

Julia let Linus drive again as she pointed out the way to her office. She felt far too distracted to be anything but a hazard on the road. Her thoughts and emotions were in upheaval, especially after speaking to Fletcher Pendleton on the phone.

The man had sounded nervous. Relieved to hear from her, pleased to meet with her, but distinctly anxious. Why? Because he was planning something? Because he already had tried something and was afraid of getting caught?

She told herself not to worry too much about it. She'd meet with him and find out what he wanted. If nothing else, she could see for herself if he fit the description of the man who'd attacked her, and if she didn't feel safe approaching him, she and Linus would walk away.

Linus had already said he wasn't going to let her take any more risks. So there was no reason for her to feel frightened. She was getting closer to ending the craziness. Then she could go back to Lydia and be there for her sister until Monica was back to her usual happy self again.

The drive to her office went quickly. Some of her associates' cars were parked in the small lot behind the brick and terra cotta three-story law office converted from a townhome. Rather than take the time answering questions about why she was back so soon, she went around to the side door that led to the old servants' stairs. They reached her office door and she pulled out her key, unlocking it. Both of them slipped inside before anyone appeared.

She let out a relieved breath.

"You have a knack for clandestine ops." Linus smiled at her.

"Thanks." Julia turned her attention to the file cabinet in the corner rather than dwell on the way his compliment sent a rush of warm feelings coursing through her. "This is the drawer." She pointed to the bronze handles with their darkened antique patina. "See how these tiny marks have scraped off the finish to the bright brassy color underneath?"

Linus gave the handle a long look. "Amateur job."

"How can you tell?"

"Do you have a needle or a pin?"

Julia opened the center drawer of her desk and pulled out the emergency sewing kit she'd kept there ever since the hem on her favorite pencil skirt had started unraveling. She handed Linus the needle.

He winked at her as he took it and slipped it into the keyhole of a different file drawer. A moment later, he pulled the once-locked drawer open. "See? Not a scratch."

"Impressive. Where'd you learn to do that? Part of your royal guard training?"

To her surprise, Linus looked genuinely embarrassed. "To be honest, I didn't always work on this side of the law." He met her eyes and breathed out slowly, as though it pained him to say the words. "I went through a rebellious phase during my teens."

Julia realized his implication, though she found it somewhat difficult to believe. "You were a criminal?"

Linus hung his head slightly. "I have a criminal record."

"I thought royal guards had to have spotless records. Monica talks about the guards as though you guys are perfect."

"I'm far from perfect." Linus caught her eyes again. "Your sister doesn't know about my record. It all happened when I was a juvenile. The old head of the guard didn't check records that far back, or he'd have found it."

"What about the new head of the guard?"

"He knows. He also respects my service record and the fact that the guard is shorthanded right now, so he hasn't said anything yet."

"Yet?" Julia tried to reconcile her feelings with the circumstances. Even though her convictions told her that King Thaddeus and Queen Monica ought to know if one of their guards had a criminal record, at the same time, she feared what that might mean for Linus. What if they let him go? Who would guard her then?

Linus pinched his lips in a firm line. It took him a moment to say the words. "Jason has promised to raise the issue the next time I come up for review—which won't be until next spring, unless I do something that would prompt a review before then." He shook his head as though to shake off the ominous tone of their discussion. "It doesn't matter. Right now we need to focus on who's after you."

Julia wanted to protest, to insist that it did matter, very much so, but she didn't know how to explain why she felt so strongly—not without confessing that she preferred him to the other guards. And those were complicated feelings she wasn't certain of herself.

Besides, Linus seemed eager to change the subject. "None of the other drawers were tampered with?"

She let him redirect their conversation. "Not that I could tell. There were no other marks or broken locks." She gave the handle in question a hard tug, and the drawer came open. "See? Whatever they did messed up the internal mechanism. This one has been loose ever since."

"But it wasn't loose before?"

"Definitely not. These drawers came with the office. They can be pretty hard to open, even unlocked. I spent my first couple of months here getting used to opening them. I sometimes needed help."

"Who helped you?"

"Other lawyers. Whoever was around. Usually Doug Palmer or Scott Gordon from across the hall." She pulled a framed picture from the shelf. Taken at the law office Christmas party, the enlarged snapshot showed everyone involved in their practice. "Doug—" she pointed to the salt-and-pepper-haired older lawyer "—and Scott." The younger man was closer to her age.

Linus looked at the picture for a long moment. "Do Doug and Scott know how you arrange your files?"

She nodded and pointed to the label on the drawer front. "Each case has a name. I keep them alphabetized."

"Very straightforward," Linus said musingly. "Does anyone else have keys to your files?"

"No. Each lawyer has a unique set of file cabinets with their own key. I keep mine on my key ring. I would have had them with me."

He nodded slowly. "If they'd had a key, they wouldn't have scraped up the lock or broken the mechanism. What about a key to your office?"

"The secretary has a spare key to all the offices. She keeps them on a set of hooks inside a cabinet of her credenza. We all know where they are."

"And your door didn't show any sign of forced entry."

"Not that I noticed. But then, I didn't realize anything was amiss until I saw the violet." At that reminder she turned to her windowsill, but of course, the plant wasn't there. She'd taken it home for Mary to water with the others. From what she'd seen of the toppled pots and dirt, the cheery flowers that had brought her so much joy were now crushed.

Her thoughts on her ravaged plants, Linus caught her by surprise with his next words.

"So, one of your coworkers could have used the spare key to enter your office. They would have known which drawer to search, but they would have had to break into the drawer. Correct?"

Julia stared at him, trying to come to terms what he was suggesting. "One of my fellow lawyers?" She looked at the picture she still held between them and examined the smiling faces of her peers.

Was the break-in at her office connected to the attacks in Lydia and the damage at her home? Could one of these people—who she worked alongside and trusted—really have acted so violently?

With newly opened eyes, Julia examined the picture of the eighteen people she worked with at the practice. The tallest men stood in the back row. She wondered if any of them were six-foot-two, or close to it. Probably three or four of them, though she'd never thought much about their heights before. She might pay more attention in the future.

She let out a long breath and finally admitted, "Yes. Any of the people in this picture could have entered my office and broken into this file. But why would they?" She met his eyes.

Linus looked at her apologetically. "I don't know why anyone would want to hurt you." His voice was soft, caring. Maybe even the tiniest bit in awe of her.

Why would Linus be in awe of her? She searched his face, wondering if she'd misunderstood. If anything, she was in awe of him. If it hadn't been for Linus, she'd have been carried off from the Lydian beach. A shudder raced through her at the memory.

Linus saw her shiver. For a moment, he looked as though he was about to extend his arms, to draw her against him.

She'd welcome that.

But instead, he broke her gaze and turned to the files. "Your attacker mentioned wanting a file. Let's look in the file drawer."

"Yes." She pushed back the longing to be held by him, and instead pulled open the drawer. Everything she had on the Seattle Electronics case was inside a file in the drawer, along with many other cases she'd covered that began with similar letters.

She flipped through the files, providing Linus with a concise summary of each until her fingers touched the *Seattle Electronics vs. Pendleton* file. "I suppose we should scour the contents?"

"Please."

Julia laid out the file on her desk, pulling out the contents and explaining each one. "Here's the engine design in question." The document was pages and pages long, with a complicated blueprint attachment dizzying in its complexity. There were more pages of the patent information, along with a copy of Fletcher Pendleton's contract which specified that everything he designed for Seattle Electronics was owned by Seattle Electronics. "Here's a brochure about Motormech." The glossy full-colored pamphlet slipped easily between the pages.

Linus picked it up and paged through it. "Motormech is a huge company. Wouldn't they know better than to try to buy a design from one of Seattle Electronics's engineers? Or did Pendleton approach them under the understanding that he owned the rights?"

"I never thought to ask who started it." Julia shook her head, wishing she'd been more suspicious then. But she'd been new to the practice and so focused on all the legal details of the case that she hadn't thought about the larger story. Maybe she could ask Pendleton about it when they met with him that evening. She glanced at the clock and sighed. "We should get moving if we're going to meet my parents."

"Can we take this file with us?"

"Sure." She scooped them up. "You can look these over. I can drive this time—I need something else to think about to get my mind off all this."

"Sure thing." He took the file as she handed it to him. "Julia?" He asked as she pushed the file drawer closed.

"Hmm?"

"You're handling this all very well."

She wasn't sure what to make of his words.

Linus added, "You're going to get through this just fine."

Much as she appreciated his kind words, she was still processing all that she'd learned, including the revelation that the guard who seemed so perfect had a criminal past. "I sure hope so."

SEVEN

"Do you think it's wise to let my parents help us at the house?" Julia asked as they neared her home. "I don't want to put them in danger."

Linus could hear the fear in her voice and wished to calm her, but at the same time, he couldn't ignore the danger of returning to the house—especially now that they'd let on to Fletcher that Julia was back in town. If Fletcher suspected anything about their meeting plans that night, he might try to strike ahead of time.

But Linus saw no need to scare Julia with that possibility. There was nothing to be gained by letting her get upset. He tried to assuage her fears. "There's strength in numbers. Whoever broke into your house has already left, and they're not likely to return with the four of us here. Besides, if the intruder has been watching the place, then they'll know the police came by once already. They ought to think twice about approaching us for fear that the police might return." Even as he spoke, Linus realized how hollow his reassurances sounded. The simple truth was, the house wasn't completely safe. But until they caught whoever was after her, no place would be safe.

He'd just have to be extra watchful.

"My folks are already here." Julia's voice trembled slightly as they pulled up to the house.

"Are you sure you're ready for this?" Linus asked.

"Not really," she admitted, "but waiting won't help anything." As Julia climbed from the car, her mother met her with a hug, followed by her father, who embraced her, as well.

Linus approached slowly, giving them space. He'd seen Dr. and Mrs. Miller when they'd visited Lydia previously, but they hadn't been formally introduced. Julia took a step back and made the introductions.

Richard Miller's hand closed over his as he pumped his arm with a firm grip. "I hear you saved my daughter's life. Thank you."

"Just doing my job."

Sheila Miller stood by her husband. "We're so very glad you did. I've been so worried about both my girls." The doctor's wife looked as if she might cry.

"We're going to get everything sorted out," Linus assured her quickly, wishing he had a more concrete guarantee to give her.

He trailed the family into the house and offered to take care of the rotting food in the kitchen. It wasn't the most likely spot to find a clue, but he wouldn't know what was out of place or missing, and he didn't want Julia dealing with the nasty mess. Besides, the intruder had avoided the front door before—it was in full view from the street. An attack would most likely come from the well-shaded rear of the property. By cleaning up the kitchen, Linus positioned himself between the Millers and the most likely line of attack.

While he cleaned, he couldn't help hearing the Millers' conversation in the next room. Sheila Miller was as concerned about Monica as Julia had been, and wanted an update from her daughter on how the newly crowned queen was faring.

"I'm so worried about her." Julia's voice was full of regret.

"I was supposed to be in Lydia making this transition easier for her. Instead I've given her more to worry about."

"You didn't choose this," her father consoled her.

"I know, Dad. But I've got to make it stop. I keep thinking about Monica and how radiant she looked the day she and Thaddeus renewed their wedding vows. I want the world to see her that way."

"They will, Julia," Sheila said with forced confidence, then made a sound that was nearly a giggle. "You don't think she's pregnant, do you?"

"Monica?" Julia sputtered. "She and her husband have only been reunited for a little over two months after six years apart."

"It's possible. She was pregnant with Peter after only being married for a matter of weeks."

"True, but don't you recall how vibrant she looked when she was pregnant with Peter? And that was even with her husband gone into hiding, and Monica not telling anyone about him."

"That's right." Sheila sighed. "Maybe I'm just eager to have more grandchildren."

There was a slight pause, and then Linus heard Julia's almost-exasperated voice. "Don't look at me! I'm in no position to bring a child into the world." A hint of desperation carried through the last of her words, and Linus could imagine her looking at the chaos inside her house, and wondering how she'd ever get her life back on track so she could move forward.

He wanted so much to help her get her life back. She didn't deserve all the trouble that had come her way.

"We'll get this mess cleaned up," Richard Miller assured his daughter. "And we'll keep praying. We got Peter back," he referred to the young prince being kidnapped by Lydia's enemies at the start of the summer and held for two days before they'd brought down the conspirators who'd taken the boy. "God will bring us safely through this trial, as well."

Linus felt the challenge behind Julia's father's faithful words. He, too, wanted to give Julia her life back. They'd be meeting with Fletcher Pendleton in a matter of hours. And then?

Maybe then they'd have some answers.

"Where is he?" Julia's impatience increased as they circled the park for the sixth time. She checked her watch. Fletcher Pendleton was over fifteen minutes late.

If nothing else, they were getting some decent exercise after sitting on their flight and in the car. But the sun dipped low in the west, and bats began to circle overhead. She'd been nervous enough about meeting the eccentric engineer in daylight.

She didn't want to face him in the dark. How would Linus be able to tell if Pendleton's eyes were the right shade of brown if it was too dark to see the man clearly?

"That's the third police cruiser that's gone past," Linus noted.

"Good. Maybe if they're patrolling the area, they'll be nearby if we have to call for help."

"I think they're headed somewhere. They've all gone that direction."

"Pendleton's house is that way." Julia stopped walking and looked up at Linus. She still had the engineer's address among her records and had selected the park in part because it was close to where he lived. But why were police cars swarming that direction?

Linus looked wary. "Why don't we swing by Pendleton's house?"

"Good idea." Julia hurried back to the car, telling herself there was no connection and no reason for haste. There were dozens of houses along those streets. The cruisers could be headed to any of them or none of them. And yet, her heart had started thumping with such force that she struggled to get the key in the ignition of the car.

Linus leaned toward her and touched his fingers to her hand. "Lord, protect us and keep us safe. Amen."

His bass voice rumbled with steady reassurance, and Julia's fingers stilled their trembling enough for her to start the car. "Thank you for that prayer. I'm starting to fall in love with that Psalm. Which one did you say it was?"

"The twenty fifth."

"I wonder how the rest of it goes."

Linus's low chuckle caught her off guard.

"What?" She glanced at him as she turned onto the long street that bore the same name as Pendleton's address. A few blocks more and they'd be there.

"I could almost recite it for you," Linus explained, but his voice tensed as they neared Pendleton's house.

Police cruisers sat silent in the street, their lights piercing the night.

"Which house?" Julia asked.

"Eighty-two fifty-three, eighty-two fifty-five," Linus read the numbers of the houses as they slowed to a stop short of the house where the cruisers sat.

"That's got to be Pendleton's house." Julia watched in horror as an officer took a roll of yellow crime scene tape and cordoned off the yard. "Oh, no," she nearly groaned, turning to Linus in vain hope that he might tell her she'd misinterpreted what she saw.

But the frustration in Linus's brown eyes told her he feared the same thing.

A middle-age couple hovered on the sidewalk in front of the house next to Pendleton's, peering from a distance at the activity beyond the crime tape.

"I'm going to find out if they know anything." Linus gestured to the couple. "Want to come?"

"Sure." Julia wasn't eager to hear what she feared the couple might tell them, but she needed answers. And she didn't want to be alone in the car, especially not with the foreboding activity that was unfolding like the yellow crime tape in front of them.

Fortunately, the woman on the sidewalk seemed bursting to tell what she knew.

"Noreen called it in. She heard the shots," the woman began without preamble, pointing to a salty-haired woman who stood near the rear garage, deep in conversation with one of the police officers.

"Shots?" Julia clarified, her stomach sinking.

"Yes. Three of them. She was in her kitchen when she heard them. When she came out to see, a car drove off. Had me on the phone by then. I told her to call the police."

"Did she get a look at the car?" Linus asked.

"Blue Toyota."

"Any idea of the model or year?"

"I don't think Noreen knows her cars enough to say model or year. She couldn't see the plates, either, because the bushes were in the way," the woman explained. "Then she went to see if Fletcher was all right and found his body by the back door."

"No!" Julia had feared as much since the moment she'd seen the police at Fletcher's house, with no sign of the engineer himself. Still, she shook her head slowly and fought against the denial that rose up inside of her. Fletcher couldn't be dead. How were they ever going to learn why he'd wanted to meet with her? How could he answer her questions if he was dead?

Unanswered questions flooded her thoughts with a cascade of dread. She'd feared Fletcher had wanted to harm her, but if he'd been murdered, that didn't likely mean she'd be safe now. No, it likely meant Fletcher hadn't been the one after her at all. Had the same party been after them both? Was that why Fletcher had wanted to meet with her?

The middle-age man had been glowering the whole time the woman told her story. Now he spoke, though Julia only listened with half an ear, as if everything was happening on a television program she wasn't sure she wanted to watch anymore.

"It's a shame, but maybe now all this nonsense will end," the man pronounced.

"What will end?" Linus clarified.

"Police here all the time." The man waved his hand at the cruisers as if to erase them.

"The police have been to Fletcher's house before?"

"Oh, yes," the woman explained. "I didn't understand why at first. I tried to get Fletcher to explain it to me. He said he thought someone had broken into his house, but nothing was taken. Just a few little things out of place. I thought he was going off his rocker. His eyes looked shifty, like a crazy person. The whole thing gave me the creeps."

The man grunted. "But the last couple times whoever broke into his house tore the place apart. He had to buy new furniture. When they broke in again, they sliced that up, too. I bought a new security system for my house, but no one's ever bothered us."

"I think they were after Fletcher, dear." The woman placed her hand on the man's arm. "I think they finally got what they were after."

"Maybe." The man didn't seem the least bit comforted. "They went to a whole lot of trouble to get it. What's this going to do to property values in the neighborhood?"

More curious onlookers approached, and the couple shuffled over to meet them and repeat their story. Julia turned to Linus. She couldn't keep the fear from her face. Her office had been disturbed, but nothing taken. Then her house was ransacked. Fletcher's experiences had followed a similar pattern.

Was Fletcher's murderer going to come after her next?

"Let's get back in the car." Linus took her arm and turned her back toward the vehicle.

She didn't realize how much she needed his support until she tried to take a step. She wavered unsteadily and Linus wrapped an arm around her waist to prop her up.

The warmth of his touch stilled the cold dread inside her. She looked up and met his eyes, grateful to have him there. In spite of his revelation about his criminal past, she trusted Linus completely. Right now he was the only thing keeping her from melting into a sobbing puddle.

"I can drive," he offered, taking the keys she still gripped in one hand.

"Thank you." She sank into the passenger seat as he lowered her gently down.

"I'm not going anywhere in particular," Linus confessed as he turned onto a busier street.

"That's okay. I don't want to head to my parent's house. What if Fletcher's murderer—" Her voice caught, and she found she couldn't muster up any more words.

Linus cast her a commiserative glance before returning his attention to the road. "The neighbor said the killer fled in a blue Toyota. I don't see a car like that right now, but I'll keep my eyes open in case one starts to follow us. In the meantime, can you get on your phone and look up the flights to and from Lydia in the next twenty-four hours?"

"Sure." Julia felt grateful to have something to do besides sit there and worry. "What are you thinking?"

"I'm thinking you need a double guard 24/7. Either we need to get some more guards over here, or you and I need to get back to Lydia where you'll have some protection."

Though going to Lydia hadn't kept her completely out of

harm's way the first time around, Julia nonetheless felt drawn to the idea. If her attackers had taken the next flight out of Lydia, they could have made it to Fletcher's house in time to pull the trigger. If she and Linus left quickly, maybe they could stay one step ahead of whoever was after her. She'd be safe—if only for the time it took until the next flight arrived in Lydia.

She pulled up the flight information, but as the words and numbers filled the screen, another thought occurred to her. "Linus?"

"Yeah?"

"Scott drives a blue Toyota."

Linus clenched the wheel a little harder, imagining the smiling face of Julia's fellow lawyer from the staff picture in Julia's office. The man would have been able to break into Julia's office easily. He had access, but what might his motives be? "Did Scott ever interact with Fletcher that you know of?"

"I don't think so. The case settled out of court. It was all very straightforward—that's why they assigned it to me even though I was new." She pressed her fingertips to her temples and shook her head. "I can't imagine how Scott would be involved, or what anyone's motive might have been for killing Fletcher."

"I can't imagine the motive for the attacks against you," Linus said, "but I don't think we're going to stop them until we figure it out."

"So, now what? Should we drive to Scott's house and see if he's home?"

"That almost sounds like a decent plan, but I don't think it would prove anything either way. He's had plenty of time to get home by now, and even if he's not home, that doesn't tell us anything." He wasn't sure exactly what they would do other than get a look at the man. If Scott had been one of

Julia's attackers, there was only the slightest possibility he would recognize him or recognize the bruises he'd given him. More than likely they'd just be walking into trouble. His goal was to keep Julia safe, not to endanger her further.

He struggled to find an answer. "Do you think we should call the police?"

"And tell them what? One of my associates drives a blue Toyota, so we think he might have killed Fletcher? Do you know how many blue Toyotas there are in Seattle?"

"Almost as many as there are men who wear size twelve shoes," Linus said with a sigh. The duchess was right. There wasn't any point calling the police. They didn't really have anything to tell them.

Julia returned her attention to her phone. "There's a connecting flight to Lydia leaving in a little over two hours with two remaining seats available."

"Book it." Linus realized he sounded as though he was giving the duchess an order, so he softened his tone and explained, "I don't want anyone reserving those seats while we think about it. I need to get you out of town. This whole mess is spiraling out of control." He clamped his mouth shut before he could say anything more that might frighten Julia. Whatever they were up against, their opponent wasn't above killing.

"Turn down this street until the next intersection." Julia pointed as she finished booking the flight over the phone. "Then follow the signs to the airport."

He turned the car toward the airport. "I think you should urge your parents to take the next flight to Lydia."

"I agree." Julia sounded almost relieved that he'd suggested it. "Monica would insist on it if she knew what was going on."

"How much do you want to tell her?"

"As little as possible, for now. There's nothing she can do about it. She'd only worry." Julia's voice cracked.

Linus wasn't sure what he should do or say. His instinct was to pull her into his arms and comfort her, but fortunately he was driving, so that wasn't an option. Besides, now that she knew about his past, she probably wouldn't want him touching her. She hadn't brought up his revelation, but he didn't have to ask. He could imagine how much a lawyer would look down on a criminal. He should be glad she still let him guard her.

Her next words surprised him. "Can you recite that Psalm?"

"Psalm twenty-five?"

"You said you had it memorized."

"That's right." Linus kicked himself for admitting as much, especially when he wasn't entirely certain he really did know all the words by heart. But he couldn't refuse Julia's request, especially if God's Word might bring her some comfort. So he began slowly, and couldn't help praying the ancient words in his heart as he spoke them aloud.

"I offer my prayer to You, O Lord. My God, I trust in You. Save me from my enemies. Those who trust in You are not defeated, but those who rebel against You are defeated."

Linus glanced at Julia just briefly before returning his attention to the road. She had her eyes pinched shut, and her face lifted up, lit by the glow of the streetlights they passed. Though he'd feared he might not remember them all, the words poured from his soul as though he'd always known them.

"I lift my eyes to the Lord, who sets me free from the traps laid for me." When he glanced at Julia again, he saw she had a tear tracing a wet line down her cheek. He faltered. Should he brush the tear away, or just ignore it?

Before he could decide, he reached the end of the Psalm. The airport lay ahead. Linus let out a long sigh. He'd been drained by all that had happened that day and the emotions the scripture had stirred up inside him.

"That is so beautiful. Thank you." Julia sniffled and pulled a tissue from her purse, swiping at the tears and clearing her throat. "Thank God you're here with me." She moved her hand, brushing the tops of his fingers where he held the steering wheel.

Though her touch was fleeting, its effects lingered, burning through him along with her words. He knew the events of the day had been particularly trying. She had to be at the end of her emotional reserves. That explained why she expressed such gratitude to have him near.

Certainly it wasn't anything more personal than that.

Was it?

EIGHT

Julia sagged into a seat to wait for their flight to be called. They'd made it through security. She'd called her parents and explained why she wouldn't be staying at their house that night, as well as urging them to head to Lydia soon.

They'd been concerned. They'd also agreed with Julia that they didn't want to share anything more with Monica than they had, too. No sense making the new queen worry more.

Julia plunked her carry-on into the empty seat beside her and stared at it thoughtfully, wondering if the file inside held any answers.

"Are you going to be okay if I step away for a moment?" Linus asked, looking around as if the couple with the whiny toddler or the nun in the next row of seats might pose some hidden threat.

Julia glanced around the terminal at their fellow travelers. "I should be fine," she assured him.

But as he walked away, she felt the tiniest bit depleted by his absence. She'd grown so used to his protective presence. What would she do if he was removed from the guard because of some long-ago criminal record? She'd been so caught off guard by his confession, and silenced by his obvious embarrassment, that she hadn't probed any deeper into the nature of his convictions.

What had he done that was so bad he could be fired because of it?

Should she be afraid of him? Maybe she ought to feel apprehensive around him, but Linus had such a gentle spirit in spite of his imposing stature. He was a Christian man of integrity and conviction—she knew that as much from his actions as she did from the way he'd recited the Psalm. He was a great guard. It wouldn't be fair for him to lose his position on the basis of something he'd done so long ago.

Julia felt something wet on her cheek and realized a tear had leaked from her eye. Brushing it away, she chided herself. How foolish! Even if she was exhausted and under a great deal of stress, what with having been attacked and a murderer probably after her—that still wasn't any reason to get weepy at the thought of Linus leaving her side.

She'd nearly schooled herself into emotional ambivalence by the time Linus returned.

He held out a bottle toward her.

She blinked at the label before recognizing her favorite flavored water.

"Don't worry, I didn't have to fight anyone for it this time." He grinned at her.

"Thank you." Julia heard the emotional hitch in those two words and clamped her mouth shut as she took the beverage he'd brought for her. She downed half the bottle before she felt steady enough to speak again. "That was very thoughtful of you. I was getting thirsty."

"You have to keep your strength up. We should both try to rest on this flight."

Julia nodded, but her throat had swelled up again. Linus was so thoughtful, so caring…so perfect. She stared at the bottle in her hands, further evidence that Linus was a nice guy, whatever the record from his past might say.

Linus took the seat next to hers. She wanted to reach for

him, or even meet his eyes and feel the connection of their shared burden, but he wouldn't look her way. Instead, he scanned the terminal, alert for possible danger.

It was his job. She knew that. But at the same time, it felt like he was purposely putting up a wall. What was he thinking? What did he feel? He'd brought her a drink. It was kind, thoughtful. But then, from what she knew of the man, he was kind and thoughtful to everyone. It wasn't as though he felt anything special for her.

How would he react if he knew about her growing feelings for him? He'd probably be horribly embarrassed, but ever the gentleman, he'd find a way to let her down gently.

She wasn't about to put him in that spot. Her life was already in upheaval. She didn't need to add to that. They'd be in Lydia soon enough, and then she'd be back in a regular rotation of guards. She wouldn't even be around him very often. Until then, she'd just have to keep her feelings under wraps.

Linus lifted Julia's carry-on bag toward the overhead compartments.

"Wait." Julia touched his shoulder. "Do you think we—" She paused, shuffled to the side as another passenger squeezed past and then met his eyes with that expression he'd seen before—the one that seemed to apologize for feeling slightly foolish.

But she only wore that expression when she was following her instincts, and he trusted whatever impulse might have prompted her to ask him to pause.

He eyed the compartment opening. Like everything else in the economy class section, it was no bigger than it absolutely needed to be. And the fat *Seattle Electronics vs. Pendleton* file made Julia's carry-on bag bulge to the side.

"Why don't we pull out the file?" Linus rested the bag on

the arm of his seat. "That way we can review it during the flight."

"Good idea." Relief and appreciation filled her face, along with something he was hesitant to name.

If he'd been a casual observer watching the duchess interact with any other man, he'd have said that look was one of admiration—more than that, of attraction. But he wasn't any other man. He was her bodyguard, and Julia had no cause to look at him like that. He was only doing his job.

Julia took the file from him and squeezed into her seat while he zipped her bag shut again and safely stowed it above. She balanced the file on her knees, watching it apprehensively as though it might hurt her.

Though Linus couldn't be sure, he suspected the contents already had hurt her. They may have even gotten Fletcher Pendleton killed.

He wanted to know why. "What do you think?" he asked with a nod to the file, the printed *Seattle Electronics vs. Pendleton* label looking as innocent as any other, except that it bore the name of a man who'd been murdered.

Julia bunched her face up as though she was trying not to cry. "I don't know. I don't even know for sure that the man on the beach really said *file*. I don't know if this is what they're after. I've already looked through it and didn't find anything. What am I looking for?"

"I don't know. Maybe a fresh set of eyes would help. Mind if I take a look?"

"Please." Julia sounded relieved to be rid of the burden.

Linus leaned back in his seat and opened up the file. A color pamphlet about Motormech caught his eye, and he opened it to read about the company's environmentally friendly innovations.

"You ever meet this guy?" Linus showed a picture to Julia. "Todd Martin, the Motormech CEO?"

Julia glanced at the picture of the robust, blue-eyed businessman, and shook her head. "Never met him, but he sounds like a great guy, always involved in philanthropic pursuits."

"He seems young for a CEO."

"He built the company by merging smaller failing companies. Saved lots of people's jobs and all that. Whatever mess this is with Seattle Electronics, I hope it doesn't end up reflecting poorly on Todd Martin. From what I understand, his innovations have moved the entire automotive industry toward greater efficiency." She pointed to the thick pages of the brochure. "It's got his story somewhere in there."

Linus found the narrative and tried to absorb the names of the various companies Todd Martin had saved over his tenure at Motormech, but the list was long and he didn't recognize any of the names. He tucked the brochure back into the file.

Reluctant to pull out too many papers when the plane would be taking off before long, Linus peered inside the file, flipping through random pages, hoping something might jump out at him.

Julia looked over his arm at the papers, and her voice held a note of sadness when she spoke. "Doesn't look like anything worth killing over, does it?"

"Not to me. But the man whose name is on the case is now dead, and this is your only link to him, so there's got to be a clue here somewhere."

Julia raised a doubting eyebrow. "I read through this file the first time the file cabinet was broken into. I couldn't find a motive then, and I still can't see one now."

Linus flipped through the pages. "All I see are white pages, black letters...and faded grayish streaks."

"Those are from the drum on my printer. One of these days I'm planning to look up how to clean that off and get rid of them, but I haven't had time."

"You've been busy," Linus noted, flipping back to get a

closer look at some of the pages he'd flipped past. "You must have fixed it at some point. These papers don't have the gray streak."

Julia peered over his arm to where he pointed. "They should. Those are the design specs for the engine. Pendleton emailed me his entire file, and I printed it all off together. See? Only these few pages here don't have the streaks. The rest of them do."

Linus felt his heart rate kick up a notch. "Why these few? Do you think it was a fluke?" He pulled out the papers and spread them across their laps, half expecting the gray streaks to appear if he held them at the right angle.

"No." Julia covered her mouth with one fist as her words descended in a horrified spiral toward despair. "Oh, no, no, no, no, no."

"What?" Linus saw the misery in her eyes and scooped the pages back together. "What is it?"

It took her a second to speak. Then she pointed at the top page with a trembling hand. "See that little smudge in the margin?"

Linus inspected the blotch, which was less than a millimeter in diameter, and not very dark. "What is it?"

"It's an imperfection on the glass of the main copier in Joan's office. I've seen it a thousand times."

"So, these pages were copied on the secretary's copy machine?" He wasn't entirely certain why that thought had Julia so distressed, but it sent a cold inkling racing along his skin.

"Yes. What time is it?"

"A little after ten."

"Good. There's still time. Have they told us to turn off electronic devices?" Julia pulled out her phone and punched a button. "Joan's a night owl."

"What are you doing?" Linus placed one hand over Julia's fingers to stop her from sending the call.

Julia froze. "I'm calling Joan. She can give us the entire copy-code history. She can tell us who used the office copier the weekend of the break-in."

"But, what if she did it?"

Julia lowered her phone and met his eyes. "Joan?"

"Yes. Isn't she the main person who uses the copier?"

"Of course she is. That's why she can find the codes to tell us who else used it." Julia sounded impatient.

Linus couldn't let her rush in to make a call she might regret. "But what if she's involved? We don't want to alert her to what we've figured out."

"Joan?"

"Yes, Joan. Or Scott, or Doug, or *someone*. Somebody is behind this—probably someone from your office with a code for the copier and access to your files. Somebody killed Fletcher. They've already come after you in various ways."

"Why do you think they killed Fletcher tonight?" Julia's voice trembled. "They'd bothered him before, obviously, but what flipped their switch from burglary to murder? Do you think, when I called Fletcher earlier today—" She swallowed hard, and tears filled her voice. "Do you think that's what set them off?"

All day, Linus had fought against the urge to comfort Julia. She needed him now. She looked at his hand close to hers. Now he gave her fingers a gentle squeeze. "Listen, Julia— nothing about Fletcher's death was your fault. Whoever has been after Fletcher must have had a reason for not killing him sooner, but if they were planning this, whether you called him today or something else happened tomorrow, he was mixed up in something you didn't start. Your phone call didn't cause his death. It was already going to happen."

Julia sagged toward his shoulder as she fought a hard battle against the tears that seemed so determined to fall. She gulped air and looked up at him. "Fletcher died because he got mixed up in this." She blinked and worked her mouth against the distasteful words. "*I'm* mixed up in this. Am I next?"

"No." Linus slid one arm around her, as if by holding her tight enough he could keep their anonymous enemies from tearing her away from him. "Nothing's going to happen to you." It was a promise he knew he wasn't qualified to make, but what else was there? He had told himself not to hold her either, yet he couldn't bring himself to let go—not when she clung to him like she needed him.

"So, what are we going to do?" She sniffled after a long pause.

As if in answer, the flight attendant began her preflight speech.

"Turn off your electronic devices," Linus whispered.

Julia looked down at Joan's number and turned off the phone. "I hope that was the right choice."

"We change planes in Atlanta. Let's try to sort through what we know. If we decide then to get in touch with Joan, you can text her while we're on the ground. In the meantime, explain to me how these copier codes work. I need to understand what you think happened."

"It's simple. All the lawyers have a printer in their office. Most documents we print in our offices. When we need copies of an original document, we use our codes on the main copier. Each lawyer has their own code. Joan can access the copier record of who prints how many copies and when."

As she spoke, Linus flipped through the file again, past the pages with the gray streaks, to the few with the tiny smudge. "These pages are numbered consecutively."

"Exactly. When I printed them off, they all had streaks from the drum on my printer. Somebody pulled out my pages with the streaks and got rid of them. They made copies of another set on the central copier, and replaced them with these. That's why these don't have gray streaks, but they're still numbered the same way."

"So, the intruder knew what they were doing. They knew the numbers on the pages they wanted to swap out. Assuming the copies were made the same weekend as the break-in, you're suggesting the intruder brought his own originals, made copies on Joan's copier, and then put those copies in the file?"

"Precisely."

"But why make the copies?" Linus couldn't sort out the reasoning behind it. "Why not just replace the pages with their originals?"

Julia touched the pages and smiled a wry smile. "As part of our commitment to environmental causes, our office uses only 100 percent post-consumer recycled paper. It has a slight greenish tinge to it. If he wanted to make everything look the same, he'd need to copy his documents onto the office paper."

"Ah, now I understand. I suppose I should have let you call Joan."

"No, you were right to stop me. I can't be certain that she's not involved in this somehow. Besides that, when I called Fletcher—" she swallowed "—well, he was murdered after I talked to him. Maybe I can figure out a way to text Joan and ask who made copies that night, without letting on to why I'm asking."

Another confusing element irked him. "What's the difference between these pages and the ones you printed off on your computer?" He couldn't make much sense of the complex engine design specifications.

"I don't know. They all look the same to me."

"So why go to all the trouble—"

"Wait." Julia grabbed his wrist and leaned closer still. "The file." She pointed to the stack of papers with her other hand. "I printed those pages off from the file Fletcher sent me. *The file.*"

Linus nodded solemnly, repeating the words she'd heard on the beach. "I don't want to have to hurt you. I just need the file." His breath caught as he stared into her wide eyes. "Do you still have the email from Fletcher?"

"I should. I never delete anything."

Linus looked down at her phone, which she'd turned off.

She looked at it as well. "I can check my email files over the phone. How long are we on the ground in Atlanta?"

"A little over an hour. That should give you time to text Joan and check your messages."

Julia still held his arm at the wrist, but now she slid her hand toward his until their fingers laced together. "Pray," she requested in a small voice, "that we'll have time and that we'll find what we're looking for and end this."

Linus didn't hesitate. As the plane took off into the night sky, he held Julia's hand secure in his and prayed that God would see them through everything, and keep the duchess safe.

By the time they reached Atlanta, Julia had decided precisely how to word her request to Joan. She sent a message asking the secretary to let her know who had used the copier the weekend of the break-in and how many copies each person had made.

With that much taken care of, Julia scrolled back through her old saved email files. "It's not there," she concluded unhappily after scrolling through several pages of messages from two years before.

"What do you mean? You can't access your old emails from your phone?"

"No, I can. I did. I've found all sorts of other things from that time period, even a few other emails related to that case, but nothing from Fletcher."

"Nothing?" Linus sounded as suspicious as she felt. "Where did they go?"

"At some point, someone must have logged into my email account and deleted it. *I* certainly didn't delete it. I save everything, remember? Besides, if I wanted to get rid of something, I'd have deleted a lot of these other frivolous messages long before I'd trash an important file."

Linus wanted to be certain he understood how her email account worked. "How could someone else log into your email? They could have done that from any computer?"

"If they had my password."

"How could they have gotten your password?"

Julia shook her head. "I check my email all the time. They could have watched me log in at a coffee shop, at the library— any time I logged in, if they were standing close enough to see my fingers hit the keys—"

"Or if they recorded an image of your fingers striking the keys—"

"Anyone with a telephoto lens could have captured me logging in through the window to my office at home, then picked through the images until they had all the keystrokes in order." She let out a frustrated huff of air, then clicked a few keys.

"What now?"

"I'm changing my password so they can't get in again." She hesitated. "Alpha numeric," she murmured, then looked up at him. "When's your birthday?"

"October twenty-fifth."

"What year?"

He told her.

She smiled a rather sweet smile. "You're two years older than I am." Then she punched the numbers into her computer. "And you're my new password."

"Are you sure you'll remember that?"

"Will you?"

"Yes, but it's my birthday. And anyway, aren't passwords supposed to be private?"

"I trust you." She met his eyes.

Linus swallowed, his Adam's apple bobbing with the motion. "I have a criminal record, you know."

Julia's breath caught. "It doesn't matter."

"You don't even know what I did."

"What did you do?"

Linus looked ashamed, his stubbled chin bent sideways, half rugged, half adorable. "Stupid things."

"Like what?

"After my parents died I fell in with a rough crowd for a while. I knew how to pick locks. Breaking into things was my way of gaining acceptance. Even though I never personally stole anything, I still got caught. I could still lose my position in the guard if it comes up during a review for any future infringement."

Julia looked back down at her phone. "It's not fair. Somebody broke into my email and deleted my file. They've gotten away with it, but you're still bound by mistakes from years ago."

"They're not going to get away with it," Linus said. "We'll get to the bottom of this. If the perp had already deleted the file, why would they come after you on the beach to ask for it again? You had to download it to print it off, didn't you?"

"Yes, but did I save it?" She pinched her forehead. "My desktop computer at work has been replaced since then. I backed up all my files onto my laptop before I transferred them. If I saved the file, it might still be on my laptop—*if* I saved it."

"The laptop in your suite at the palace?" Linus confirmed.

"Yes."

"Which has been in Lydia since before the break-in at your house?"

"Yes."

Linus pulled out his phone. "If you don't mind, I'm going to call the royal guard and tell them to secure your laptop at headquarters."

"You don't think it's safe inside my suite at the palace?"

"At this point—" Linus's Adam's apple bobbed again as he swallowed "—I don't want to take any chances. I don't understand that engine design, but somebody thinks this file is worth killing over. We need to figure out why."

NINE

Julia awoke in daylight and blinked, disoriented. What day was it? They'd skipped a day during their flight, or flown right through it, the fifteen-odd hours they'd spent into the air combining with the time zones they'd passed through to make it midafternoon or so. Now she wasn't sure where they were in the air, but her dry throat and cramped legs told her she'd been sleeping on the plane for a long time. Surely they were nearly to their destination.

She took a deep breath and lifted her head, discovering to her horror that she'd slumped against Linus's shoulder at some point during her slumber.

Had he noticed? She backed away just far enough so that she could see his face.

He slept, the bruise above his eye more visible than before with his lids closed, its sickly green a sign of healing and a tiny testament to one fraction of all he'd done for her. She felt a surge of affection charge through her and a foreign tenderness at the sight of the sleeping guard. He'd brought her so much comfort since he'd been a part of her life.

There was no doubt in her mind that she wouldn't have made it this far without Linus at her side. More than that, she wished she could keep him at her side. Perhaps she could find a way to word her feelings so that Monica would request to have Linus assigned to guard her more often. Could she do that in such a way that Monica would attribute her preference to Linus's competence and not any attraction she felt for the guard?

She'd be mortified if Monica got the impression she'd fallen for the man—more embarrassed still if Linus guessed at her feelings. He'd never given her any indication that he felt anything toward her. If he knew she had feelings for him, he might feel uncomfortable guarding her.

The thought pricked her heart. What were her feelings, exactly? How was she supposed to interact with her bodyguard? Could she count him among her friends? He'd certainly been a friend to her over these past several days, but then, it was his job to keep her out of danger. She doubted anything in his job description required him to remember her favorite flavor of bottled water.

Nor was he likely required to hold her while she sobbed over her ransacked house, or to recite the twenty-fifth Psalm to her while she was afraid.

Linus had done those things out of the goodness of his heart. He had a very good heart.

If Monica asked, Julia could tell her she appreciated that Linus understood her—understood her preferences, whether it was her favorite beverage or letting her have the seat by the window on the plane. Monica would understand that much, surely.

In the meantime, she could see the Grecian islands outside her window. They'd be landing in Lydia soon. She needed to stop thinking about Linus and starting thinking about her sister. How was she ever going to explain everything to Monica without worrying her more?

Linus hoisted their carry-on bags over his shoulder. His fellow guards knew what time to expect them. Given all the threats against Julia of late, he knew they'd be ready.

Was Julia ready? She looked rumpled, her eyes haunted by the fears that dogged them. He wished he could pull her into his arms, but it wasn't his place. And there wasn't time.

Julia lingered in the seat row, staring intently at the screen on her phone.

Had she heard from Joan? Linus stepped closer.

"Joan sent me three different codes for the weekend of the break-in. Some of those could be legitimate copies, though."

"There were six pages in your file with the smudge," Linus noted. "How many copies are associated with each code?"

"One has over two hundred copies. The other two have eight and ten. Now who belongs to each code?" Julia scrolled down through the message on the tiny screen. "Scott Gordon made ten copies."

"Who made the other eight?"

"Doug Palmer."

"Doug's familiar with your files as well, isn't he?"

"Both of them are. It could be either of them."

"And they're both around six-two, one-eighty?"

Julia's face had paled, but she nodded.

"Have either of them ever mentioned any martial arts experience, military training, an interest in hand-to-hand combat, anything like that?"

Julia blew out a slow breath as she shook her head.

"We've got to narrow this down. What about the file? How much has it been handled, aside from the two of us touching it on the flight?"

"I read through everything in the file drawer, looking for any clues," Julia confessed.

"That's all?"

"All that I know of."

"That's not too much contamination. We could still find some decent prints," Linus resolved.

"Wouldn't the perpetrator have worn gloves?"

"He may have tried to. But if he had to open the file, pull out the pages that were originally there, and replace them with the copies he'd made, he may have had a very difficult time doing so using gloves. If he removed them, even in a brief moment of frustration, we could get a print, or enough of a partial print to narrow down our target between Scott and Doug." Then Linus almost laughed. "Of course, we'd need prints from Scott and Doug to do that."

"Joan can send them to us."

"Joan has their fingerprints on file?"

"The law office has everyone's prints on an electronic database. We work with too many criminal cases—you'd be surprised how often our fingerprints are needed for things. I'll text Joan and ask her to send the prints for everyone at the office."

"Great idea. I'll give you the email address for an investigators, and Joan can send the prints directly to them You can text her in the car on the way to the palace." Linus looked down the aisle and realized nearly everyone else had left the plane. "Let's get going. The other guards will be waiting for us."

As Linus had hoped, his fellow guards had arrived in force to escort the duchess safely back to the palace. Jason headed the envoy that had arrived to whisk them away. While Galen loaded their bags into the waiting car, Linus stepped closer to Jason and spoke in low tones, filling in his supervisor on what they'd learned, as well as the need to lift fingerprints from the *Seattle Electronics vs. Pendleton* file. He handed over the papers gently, praying that they hadn't obscured what few clues they might be able to find.

"You really don't have to carry that," Julia assured Linus as he hauled her bag all the way inside her suite for her. "It's not that heavy."

"Then it isn't too much of a burden for me to carry it for you." He grinned back at her.

She couldn't argue against his point—not without insulting his strength or his courtesy, neither of which she wanted to question. So she smiled resignedly and thanked him.

Returning to the palace had been emotionally draining. She'd embraced her sister and nephew and made plans to eat dinner with them in a couple of hours. Pleased as she was to see them again, she couldn't help thinking that Monica looked as though she'd lost weight. And she'd never been anything but slender to begin with.

Linus broke through her worried thoughts. "Sam's going to be your guard for the rest of this shift. You'll be sure to page him if you need anything?" He placed her bag on a bench near the door and turned to face her.

Julia smiled up at him, more than aware that she'd failed to page him the night she'd gone jogging. If she had, perhaps she wouldn't have been attacked. But then whoever was after her would have had to find a different time to strike, possibly even when her sister or nephew were nearby. The thought made her shiver.

"Are you going to be okay if I leave you now?" Linus had clearly noticed the tremble that ran through her. He lifted one hand toward her shoulder, then paused with his fingers outstretched just a few inches from her.

She looked at his hand, then at his face.

"I shouldn't touch you," he whispered.

"Why not?" she whispered back. The door to the hallway was still open, though they stood to the side, out of range of the security camera that hung in plain sight in the hall.

"It's not my place. I'm your guard. I've already gotten closer to you than I should."

Julia felt her cheeks grow warm. She wanted to let him know how she felt, but she was terrified that he might not feel the same way. Still, he had to know how much he'd helped her over the past few days. "I appreciate that you've been there for me. I wouldn't have made it otherwise."

He'd moved closer to her, almost against his own will. "In the future—" He began, but a sudden buzzing cut him off.

"My phone." Julia patted her purse, disoriented, regretting that their conversation had been interrupted. She fumbled through the bag, her fingers shaking slightly. "I wonder if it's Joan getting back to me."

"I thought she was going to email Simon and Oliver, not call you."

"I thought so, too. Knowing Joan, she's taken care of it already." Julia pulled out the phone just as it stopped ringing. "Two missed calls. I must not have heard it ringing earlier." Her voice caught as she read the number she'd entered into her phone the year before when it had been her job to help plan the company picnic along with a few of her fellow lawyers.

"Linus." She reached for his arm with trembling fingers as she held out the phone so he could see the name.

Scott Gordon.

She couldn't speak, but fortunately, she didn't have to. Linus took a step closer and slipped his arm around her waist. Whatever he'd said a moment before about not touching her, the incoming call had changed that. She sagged against him, comforted that he'd known she could use someone strong to lean on as she struggled to absorb this latest blow.

"What," she tried to speak, swallowed hard, and then attempted the question again. "What do you think he wants?"

Linus met her eyes with steady understanding. Of course he couldn't know any more than she did what Scott Gordon was after, but at least he understood the fear she felt. She could see it echoed in his eyes, along with the ready strength with which he'd met every challenge they'd encountered so far.

"I don't know." His bass voice sounded dry. "But I think we should alert the other guards before you try to return this call."

To Julia's relief, Linus didn't budge from her side as he called his fellow guards and let them know about the calls from Scott. Sam, who was assigned to guard her next anyway, was at her door by the time she and Linus stepped through it. They headed for the royal guard headquarters. Julia felt a little unsteady on her feet and a little lightheaded after this latest surprise, but she didn't want the other guards to see her leaning on Linus so she walked on her own a couple of feet away from him—close enough that he could still catch her if her injured leg gave her trouble, but far enough from him not to raise any eyebrows.

Jason, the head of the royal guard, met them before they reached the doors of the royal guard headquarters. "I think you should take a look at this."

Julia's mouth went dry at the foreboding tone of Jason's words. What now?

Jason led them into a small, well-lit room. Julia immediately recognized the papers spread out on the table, though the pages from her file were now dusted with a dark powder. Monitors above held fingerprint images.

"Your secretary was very prompt about forwarding those prints. We've got a preliminary match," Jason explained. "I wasn't going to say anything until we confirmed it, but if this guy's been trying to call you…" he said as he pointed to the distinct prints on the page.

Julia looked up from the dusted prints to those on the screen, labeled *Scott Gordon.*

"Scott made ten copies the weekend Julia's office was broken into," Linus recounted. "Then he replaced these pages in this file. But why?"

Julia met his eyes. "The file—" she shook her head "—but the break-in was *weeks* ago. Why attack me on the beach—"

"He must believe you still have copies of the original file."

"They were deleted from my email records."

Linus turned to Jason. "Did the guards secure Julia's laptop?"

"Yes. It's in the next room." Jason raised a hand to stop them as they moved toward the door. "You got a phone call from Scott—" he pointed at Julia "—where is he now?"

"Where is Scott?" Julia's voice faltered as she realized the importance of the head guard's question. "I don't know."

"We need to know."

Julia blew out a steadying breath and pulled out her phone, then hesitated. "Scott left a voice mail."

Jason and Linus exchanged looks.

"Do you have a picture of him?" Linus asked. "We can have the border authorities be on the lookout for him."

"The company website has headshots of all the lawyers along with a bio." Julia pulled a business card from her purse and pointed out the web address to Jason as she handed him the card.

"We'll get that image circulated." Jason assured them as he stepped through the door, card in hand.

Julia looked at the fingerprints once more before turning to meet Linus's eyes. "What do you think? Should I wait for them to listen to the message from Scott?"

"Can you save it after you listen to it?"

"Of course."

"Then we can always listen to it with them again. Right now I think we need to know what he had to say." Linus closed the door, closing out the noise from beyond. "Can you put it on speakerphone?"

"Sure thing." Julia pulled out her phone, but before she

touched any buttons, it began to ring. She stared at the screen, waiting for the caller ID to identify the source.

Scott Gordon.

Julia whimpered.

"Don't answer it yet. We'll wait for the rest of the guards."

"Okay." Julia was more than happy for an excuse not to have any contact with the man who suddenly wanted so much to talk with her. She waited until the phone stopped ringing, then looked at Linus. "What do you think?"

Linus shook his head slowly. "I don't know. He's my prime suspect right now."

"For the attack against me on the beach?"

"And for everything." Linus didn't say Fletcher's name out loud or mention the word *murder*. Instead he turned to face her, and his voice sounded tired, even tender. "My job is to keep you safe."

"To my understanding, you're supposed to be off duty right now. Sam's supposed to be guarding me." Julia took a step closer to him, eager to know why he felt the need to stay at her side even though his shift was over. Did he feel the way she felt? With every new thing she learned about him, her feelings for him grew.

His gaze lingered on her face for one emotion-filled moment. He spoke in a reluctant voice. "Then I suppose I should be going." Yet he didn't make a move toward the door.

Julia summoned up her courage. "What if I don't want you to go?"

Linus moved closer to her, his gaze never leaving her face. "I need to. You're the queen's sister. I'm just a guard." In spite of his words, he leaned closer as he spoke.

"You're more than just a guard to me." Julia intended her words to encourage Linus to say what he felt, but they also bordered on a declaration of her feelings.

"Julia…" Linus reached toward her face, brushing her

cheek with the whisper-soft touch of his fingertips. "I respect you."

"I respect you." She felt a hopeful smile rise to her lips.

"I can't get involved with you. If I let anything happen between us, it would prompt an immediate review of my record."

Julia felt her heart plummet. "A review. Jason would share your juvenile record."

"I can't ask him to withhold that information. If I'd have realized the old head of the guard hired me without knowing it, I'd have made it known long ago. But I didn't know then, and now is the worst possible time for anyone to find out. In the wake of the attacks against the royal family, Jason has instituted strict standards for the guards. I believe in those standards. I can't ask him to make an exception for me."

Julia regretted the fact, but she understood where Linus was coming from. "If he makes an exception for you, he'd set a precedent of making exceptions. And that could ultimately lead to a breach of security that would endanger my sister's family."

"I'm glad you understand." Linus still held his fingers alongside her face, and now cupped her cheek in his hand. "I care deeply about you. But I also care about the safety of your extended family."

Julia couldn't repress a smirk. "That only makes me like you more."

Linus smirked back and leaned closer. "It's a dangerous line of work." He hovered for a moment mere inches from her lips.

Much as she wanted to lean forward and kiss him, she understood why they couldn't allow themselves that pleasure. Still, she could hardly pull away from him.

"Jason wanted to listen to that—" Sam opened the door, then froze, looking at them.

Linus pulled back.

Julia looked shamefully toward her feet.

"—phone message," Sam ended, looking back and forth between the two of them. "Unless this isn't a good time?"

Linus clapped a hand on his fellow guard's shoulder. "It's a perfect time, thank you."

"And I'm supposed to relieve you," Sam reminded Linus.

"That's fine—" Linus smiled agreeably "—but if you don't mind, I'd like to stick around for now."

Sam hesitated and looked at Julia. "Miss Miller?"

"I'm glad to have you." Julia smiled at Linus, trying not to smirk. "Let's see if we can learn something from those phone messages."

TEN

They stepped into the hallway just as Jason came around the corner toward them. "I've contacted the cell phone tower authorities. They're going to help us locate the caller. We'll listen to the messages first. Then, if we determine it's safe to do so, we'll return Scott's calls. The cell tower authorities should be able to narrow down his location using the strength of his connection to surrounding towers."

Julia had heard of cases that used the cell tower pinging method to substantiate a caller's location. They were often able to pinpoint a location with total accuracy. And all she really wanted to know was whether Scott was in Seattle or Lydia.

Jason led them to a large conference room with a long central table. Wheeled office chairs surrounded the table, and a pot of coffee was brewing at a small kitchenette station in one corner. "Can I get you anything?" Jason asked.

"I'd take some of that coffee as soon as it's done. Thanks." She sat next to Linus and placed her phone on the table in front of her.

A couple more guards entered behind them. One of them had a recording device, and the other fiddled with the settings on her phone.

"I've got the volume all the way up," he informed Jason. "We're ready."

Jason brought her a steaming mug of coffee.

Linus leaned closer and whispered. "There's milk in the fridge."

It took Julia just a second to realize there was a small refrigerator under the counter, and to put together the fact that Linus had no doubt watched her pour milk into her coffee several times over the past few days. It was something she did without even thinking about it. But he'd thought about it.

Touched by his gesture, all she could do was nod.

Linus hopped up and brought her the milk, along with a mug of coffee for himself. By the time he'd replaced the carton back in the fridge, everyone was seated.

"We're ready," the guard who'd fiddled with her phone explained. "It's set to speakerphone so everyone can hear the messages."

"Okay." Julia entered her password to retrieve the messages, and Scott's voice filled the room.

"Hey, Julia, it's Scott. I wanted to ask you a couple questions. Can you call me back? Thanks."

Her fellow lawyer's voice sounded casual—almost forcedly casual, but she was so nervous, she might have projected the forced part. She saved the message and proceeded to the next.

"Julia. It's Scott. Did you get my message? It's actually kind of important that I talk to you, preferably soon. It's, well, it's complicated. Call me back as soon as you can, and I'll explain. Thanks."

Julia saved the message and the phone proceeded to give the date and time of the message. She wished her phone had offered her a pause-and-absorb-what-you-just-heard option, but it had only offered her delete-and-move-on or save-and-move-on, and she wasn't about to delete.

They listened to the message Scott had left moments before, after Julia hadn't answered her ringing phone. Scott's voice had a higher pitch this time. He sounded nervous, almost jumpy.

Almost like Fletcher Pendleton had the last couple of times he'd called her. It sent a foreboding ripple down her spine.

"Julia, it's Scott. I need to talk to you, preferably in person. It may be—" he paused, and she could almost hear his anxious swallow "—it may be a matter of life and death. Yours. Mine. I—I think I got in over my head. For what it's worth, I'm sorry. Please call me back as soon as you can. Bye."

Julia couldn't look at the phone any longer. She gulped a little coffee to take the dry lump from her throat, then looked at Linus, hoping he'd know better than she did what to make of Scott's message.

Linus met her eyes, but said nothing, only pulled in a long breath.

Jason leaned forward. "Let's hear those again."

"Do we have to?" Julia realized the moment she spoke the words that they sounded like a plea from a small child, but she felt very small and overwhelmed by what she'd heard—especially the eerie similarity to Fletcher Pendleton's voice, and Scott's reference to life and death.

Scott wanted to meet with her. Fletcher had wanted to meet with her. She'd refused him until it was too late, and now he was dead.

She reached forward and hit the button to replay the message.

Scott's voice hadn't lost its note of desperation.

It may be a matter of life and death. Yours. Mine. I—I think I got in over my head. For what it's worth, I'm sorry. Please call me back as soon as you can. Bye.

Julia pinched her eyes closed and wished the words weren't real. She opened her eyes to see the guards nodding in agreement around the table.

"What?" she asked, guessing at what the wordless signal meant and fearing she was right.

She was.

Linus confirmed it. "You need to call him back. The sooner you talk to him, the sooner we find out what's been going on."

Julia nodded. Linus was right—she knew it deep in her heart. It would take them forever to sort out Scott's motive on their own. They'd already admitted to one another that they had very little idea what he was involved in. They might not like what Scott was going to tell them, but at least they'd finally know something.

One of the guards plugged something into her phone. "This will record the entire conversation and transmit it so the rest of us can hear. We'll put you in the next room so Scott doesn't pick up our noises and become suspicious."

She followed the guard into the next room, wishing she had some excuse to keep Linus next to her. But no, he needed to be in the room where her conversation was being transmitted, so he could hear everything that was said.

"There's a window here." The guard moved a panel to one side, revealing a clear piece of glass through which she could see the guards sitting at the table. "If you have a question, write on the glass." He handed her a marker.

"Okay." She absorbed everything he'd said and gripped the marker in one hand, her phone in the other.

"When you're ready." The guard nodded and closed the door behind him on the way out.

Julia looked through the glass, which had a bit of an opaque tinge, so that she could see the guards clearly, and superimposed in front of them, she saw her own reflection.

She looked frightened. She took a gulp and tried to give herself a reassuring smile.

From beyond the glass, Linus met her eyes and smiled back. That simple gesture reminded her that she wasn't alone—

not really—even if he wasn't in the same room with her. He was nearby and he would keep her safe. She closed her eyes and called to mind the words of the Psalm he'd recited. *My God, I trust in you. Save me from my enemies.*

Julia opened her eyes and looked at Linus again. He had a reflective look on his face, and she was hit with the realization that he seemed to be praying—maybe even praying that very Psalm again for her. At the thought, the tension began to ease from her trembling hands. She could do this.

She lifted her phone and dialed.

Linus watched Julia's face intently as he listened to the transmission, which carried through clearly. The phone rang twice before Scott answered.

"Julia?"

"Yes. Scott?"

"Thank you for calling me back."

"What did you need?"

"Remember when your office was broken into a few weeks ago?"

"Yes."

"I think I know who did it. I mean, I don't know their names, but I sort of helped them do it. I didn't know. I thought I was helping." Scott's words ran together in a panic. "They told me not to tell anyone, not to say anything. They threatened me—my fingerprints were all over the papers. They said I'd go to jail. I'd be their scapegoat. I was stupid. I was scared. I didn't think."

"Who? What happened?"

"Two guys. They stopped by the office. I recognized them from when you worked on that Seattle Electronics case. They seemed legit. Listen, that's not the important part. The important thing is that I did some looking into it, and I figured out what they're after. Can I meet with you and show you what I found?"

"Yes." Julia sounded eager.

"I'm in Lydia. Joan told me you were here. It's important that we talk in person."

Julia didn't look too surprised to hear that Scott was nearby or that Joan had told him of her plans. They were no big secret.

"Yes. I'm here. I can meet with you." From the sound of Julia's breathless voice, Linus got a sense of the impatience she felt. If Scott had answers for them, if the thugs who'd killed Pendleton were after him, they needed to meet with him as soon as possible to learn what he knew—before Pendleton's murderers caught up to him.

Somehow the killers had known Pendleton had made plans to meet with Julia, whether by bugging his house or spying on him or listening in on his phone calls, they'd known. Either that or the time of his murder had been a great coincidence.

Linus didn't believe in coincidences. Especially not coincidences involving murder.

"Do you know your way around Lydia?" Scott quizzed Julia. "I've never been here before."

Linus wasn't sure he believed the man's claim, but Julia didn't press for specifics.

"Where are you now?"

Scott listed a downtown Sardis hotel and a room number. Julia wrote *OK?* on the window.

Linus glanced at his fellow guards. They nodded. He nodded, too.

"I can meet you at your hotel," Julia agreed. "You don't have to go anywhere. I'll get there as soon as I can. Is that okay?"

"Okay. Thank you, Julia. See you then."

Julia closed the call and placed the marker in the tray with a shaking hand.

Linus met her in the hallway.

"Is that okay?" Even her voice trembled. "Do you think we'll be okay?"

"I think we need to get to Scott as soon as we can."

"I think so, too. He sounded so much like Fletcher. If the same men are after him who were after Fletcher…"

Linus nodded. "We need to find out what he knows." He didn't mention the possibility that it might be a trap. If Scott had been faking it, he'd fooled them all. But even if they were walking into something, they weren't alone. They had the royal guard behind them this time—enough manpower to take on just about anyone.

No, Julia's instincts had been spot-on. They needed to catch up to Scott before anyone else did.

They put their plan together as they moved down the hall toward the door closest to the garages. Simon had placed a call to the hotel the instant Scott had given the name. He'd confirmed they had a guest named Scott Gordon checked in and convinced them to forward him a diagram of the hotel floor plan.

"The cell phone towers traced the call to the hotel, confirming his location." Simon grabbed the hotel floor plans from the printer tray as they passed by his office and dispensed them as they trotted toward the cars.

"Scott's room is 216, second floor, interior balcony overlooking the pool," Simon briefed them.

"Elias!" Jason trotted over and stuck his head in the guard booth by the back gate. "I need you to fly the helicopter."

An older man shuffled out. "What's the mission?"

"Surveillance. Galen can fly with you. He'll get you up to speed."

"We'll keep a low profile," Jason told the gathered guards.

There were only six of them, plus Galen who'd gone with Elias back into the building to reach the helicopter parked on the roof. "Linus, you know the duchess best. I want you in the room with her. Got that? She doesn't go in the room unless she's with you."

Linus nodded sharply and cast a glance at Julia to be certain she understood.

Everything on her face said she'd comply. She was too frightened at the moment to do otherwise.

Jason used the map to outline positions for the rest of the men. He'd pulled every man who wasn't on specific detail, leaving behind only those guards assigned to members of the royal family, and those with specific duties, such as guarding the gatehouse or overseeing the surveillance cameras. Even at that, he'd left only one man at each station.

Linus wished they had more men, but at least he knew he could trust those few they had with them. Jason had insisted on that as a cornerstone of his hiring policy, given the breach that had nearly cost the former king his life earlier that summer.

They weren't many, but they would have to be enough.

Moments later they were buckled into three cars headed downtown as quickly as the narrow roads would allow. Cold fingers slipped into his open palm.

Linus looked down and realized the duchess had taken his hand. He gave her fingers a reassuring squeeze. "It's going to be okay. We're going to find out what's been happening." He glanced at the clock on the dashboard. "You're supposed to eat with your sister in a little over an hour. I'm not expecting you to be late."

"Thank you." The car careened around a corner, and Julia leaned toward him, her eyes still fixed on his.

For an instant, Linus felt the temptation to kiss her. It

would be so easy. Her lips were so close to his already, he'd hardly have to tip his head and turn a little to the side—

He shook off the thought as the car straightened out. He couldn't kiss the duchess! Why was he even thinking such a thing, when they were so close to making a break in the case? He pinched his lips shut and stared out the window at the passing streets. He needed to get a better grip on his emotions. But that was a difficult task, what with Julia's fingers entwined with his.

They pulled to a stop under the hotel porte cochere, and Linus helped the duchess from the car while the other guards piled out behind him. The drivers zipped around the building to the parking lot, then ran back to join them.

"Head on up. Take Sam. He's in full armor," Jason instructed him. "We'll get into position."

Linus nodded. He could hear a helicopter rapidly approaching and knew that Galen would keep them informed of anything he saw from the sky. If they were walking into a trap, his fellow guards would spot the signs.

Ducking inside the revolving glass doors, Linus took a few steps toward the desk as he got his bearings, quickly recognizing the layout from the floor plan Simon had shared.

"Should we take the stairs?" Julia pointed to the graceful stairway that descended from the balcony above. "It might be faster than waiting for an elevator."

"Great idea." Linus spotted the pool beyond wide windows that separated the formal hotel entry from the casual space beyond. Scott's room overlooked the pool.

They reached the top of the steps and hurried along the balcony to the glass door that completed the pool area enclosure. A whiff of chlorine greeted him when he opened the door, but he ignored it as he read off the room numbers.

"Two-sixteen," he whispered as they came to a stop in front of it. With a quick glance around, he saw Paul, one of his men, stationed at the far end of the balcony, and another guard, Oliver, by the main hotel entrance. The other two would be outside, one at the front of the building, one at the back.

He studied the door for only a second before he decided he didn't want Julia standing in front of it. If they were walking into a trap, someone on the other side could put a bullet through the door the moment she knocked.

Pulling Julia down the hall, away from the room, Linus whispered to Sam to knock. In his full body armor, Sam would fare much better against a bullet. And if there was no threat, Julia could go in.

Sam rapped lightly on the wood. He looked at them expectantly.

Nothing.

He knocked again, this time a little harder.

Even as Sam's knuckles made contact with the door, Linus's earpiece buzzed with Galen's voice transmitted from the helicopter he could hear hovering above the hotel. "I've got two figures headed out a second-floor window. It's the eighth window from the west end—I believe that makes it room two-sixteen." Galen paused. "One of those figures has a gun. Nick, are you seeing this?"

"I'm on the ground." Nick's voice carried through in slightly hushed tones. "I see the men. There's a bit of a decorative balcony there—they look like they're going to jump. I'm holding back. I want them on the ground before they see me."

"I'm coming around the side of the building," Jason informed them next. "Liam, leave your station and bring a car around back. The rest of you, stay at your posts."

As their conversation played into his earpiece, Linus realized Scott wasn't alone. Whoever was with him had no intention of letting Scott share the information he learned. He motioned to Sam. "Kick the door in."

Linus tucked Julia tight against his chest and she pressed close, as though suspecting a violent explosion at any moment. They were down the hall from the door to 216, well out of the way of any shots that might come through the hotel room wall. He'd have kicked in the door himself, but he wasn't armed. He was technically supposed to have gone off duty after he'd delivered Julia safely to the palace, but of course that hadn't been possible.

Sam was well armored and wore steel-toed boots. He dropped the door with one kick.

"Freeze! Royal guard!" Sam shouted as the door went down.

"They're jumping," Nick reported from the ground.

"I'm after them," Jason's voice cut out.

Sam leaped inside the room. Linus thought he caught a whiff of smoke, and eased close enough to peek around the doorway just in time to see Sam lift a bed pillow from a smoldering pile of papers.

He looked up from the charred remains grimly. "They wouldn't have set those on fire if they weren't important."

The top several pages were blackened, and the edges of the all the papers had burned as well, but Linus held out hope that Sam's quick thinking had saved something, at least.

"Can I look?" Julia took a tentative step across the flattened door.

But the sound of shooting echoed through the open hotel room window, and Linus pulled her back. "I don't want you going in there. Sam, see if you can find any other evidence they might have left behind. We'll have to be careful with those papers if we're going to preserve any of the contents. I'll take Julia to the car."

Julia looked up at him as though she might protest being led away.

"You're far more important than those papers," he whispered as he led her toward the stairs.

"But we need to find out—"

"We will. We may be able to read the contents of the burned pages if they aren't disturbed. It's better this way." He wished he could assure her of more, that Jason and his men would bring in Scott and whoever was with him, but he couldn't make any promises. In fact, given the gunfire—which hadn't sounded like any of the sidearms the royal guardsmen carried—he prayed fervently that Jason and all his men would make it back, empty-handed or not.

Linus helped Julia into the car before driving them back toward the palace. His earpiece relayed his fellow guards' activities as they unfolded. Scott was down—shot by the man who'd shoved him through the window. Jason was checking his vitals while Nick and Liam went after the gunman, who'd hopped in a car waiting at the end of the alley.

Galen kept the men on the ground informed of the car's escape route. Nick and Liam sped after it, but had to pause to let the ambulance through. By the time they caught up to the vehicle, the men had ditched it and slipped among the tourists crowding the market.

"Which way did they go?" Nick demanded.

"I can't tell," Galen reported glumly from the sky. "They went under the central canopy. It's too crowded down there—they may have come back out again. Check the center stalls."

But from the transmissions Liam and Nick provided, they couldn't identify anyone inside the market stalls.

Jason didn't have any better news. "Scott was shot twice through the abdomen. He's still breathing. The ambulance arrived quickly. He may have a chance of pulling through."

Linus prayed with eyes wide open as he steered their car toward the palace. He didn't want to tell Julia what he'd heard, but when he glanced her way he saw her looking up at him expectantly.

"Did I hear an ambulance?"

He met her eyes and wished he didn't have to deliver the news.

"The shots we heard—"

"Scott was hit in the abdomen. He's still alive."

Julia pinched her eyes shut. Regret filled her face. She looked up at him again as the car pulled through the palace gates. "Do you think we caused it?"

Linus had already been pondering the same question. "No. Scott already said he was in over his head and scared. Those men may have tailed him all the way from Seattle. If they'd shot him elsewhere, we wouldn't have been around to call an ambulance. And Sam saved some of the papers, at least. That should give us a clue of what Scott had been planning to tell you."

"I should have asked him for more details over the phone. I should have learned what I could while I had the chance, but he said he wanted to meet in person."

"Maybe we'll learn more from those papers than Scott could have told you over the phone. We did what we thought was best. Don't look back and wish you'd done things differently. All we can do now is try to make the best of what we have."

He parked the car in the garage and ran around to help Julia out.

"I'm supposed to have supper with my sister in fifteen minutes. What should I tell her?"

"You don't have to tell her anything." He paused, prepared to leave her by a back door of the palace. "Sam isn't back yet, is he?"

"No, the other two cars have yet to return."

"I can escort you to your room." He opened the door for her.

"But you're supposed to be off duty."

He met her eyes as she stepped past him into the palace. "I'm not going anywhere until I'm sure you're safe."

ELEVEN

Julia felt as though Linus had wrapped a warm blanket around her with his words. From the moment she'd seen Scott's name on her phone, she'd felt shaken. Even more so when she'd heard gunfire and learned that the one man who'd offered to tell her what was going on had been shot.

But Linus had already proven himself stalwart and trustworthy. Just knowing he was with her gave her the strength to keep going.

With Linus stationed outside the door to her suite, she changed into a fresh blouse and ran a brush through her thick brown hair before stepping back out again to join him.

He smiled at her. "You look great."

She followed as he led her quickly toward the dining room, the echo of his compliment seeping through her. His words weren't fancy, but the glimmer of his eyes had told her they were sincere, and that knowledge warmed her more than anything.

Concerned as she was about having to tell Monica what had happened that afternoon, she was pleased to discover her sister was preoccupied with news of her own, which she shared the moment Julia entered the room.

"This is the announcement for your titling ceremony." Monica held up an embossed card for her appraisal.

"Sunday," Julia read the words aloud. "*This* Sunday?"

"We needed to move it up. If you don't approve we could push it back, but it really would help if we could move it forward."

"It's completely up to you," Julia assured her. "I'm just the recipient. But are you sure you want to have it so soon, with all that's been happening lately? Sunday is only four days away." They were the only two in the room, besides Linus who still hovered near the doorway. Julia wouldn't have mentioned the distressing events of late if her nephew had been present. She wasn't particularly pleased about bringing them up to her sister, but she thought it ought to be addressed.

Monica looked down at the invitation, and Julia couldn't help noticing how thin and drawn she looked. When the queen looked back at her, apology shined in her eyes. "That's actually part of the reason why we wanted to move forward. This way, there won't be time for too much commotion."

Monica's final word hung between them, implied meaning heaped upon it, full of unspoken threats.

Julia understood. The sooner they sprang the titling ceremony, the less opportunity anyone would have to plot to use the public assembly to their advantage. Clearly, Monica didn't think Julia was going to be free from the trouble that followed her anytime soon.

"Sunday will be perfect," Julia rushed to assure her. "Can Mom and Dad be here by then?"

"They're planning to arrive in Lydia tomorrow," Monica said, beaming at her with appreciation. "If you're okay with it, we'll send out the announcements. You won't have a large crowd on this short notice, but I think it will be best that way."

"Of course," Julia agreed, and tried to make her words sound sincere. "I feel so honored to have a title. A small crowd is probably best." The last thing she wanted to do was give Monica any more reason for concern. Linus and the guards had everything under control. She had to trust that, and focus on getting through dinner without letting on to her sister all that was wrong.

Peter bounded into the room as she spoke. King Thaddeus entered on the heels of his son, followed by his sisters the princesses and Prince Alec and all their fiancés. Isabelle and Anastasia hovered near, gushing about the invitation and how lovely the ceremony would be. Julia nodded, reminding herself that she hadn't expected anything, certainly not something as prominent as the title of duchess.

She should be happy.

But the cold fear knotted inside her would not be tamped down, no matter how many times she forced a smile to her lips. The royals, at least, seemed too excited by their plans to notice the tremor in her voice when she spoke, or to spot the tremble of fear in her hands.

It was Linus who leaped forward to pull out her chair while everyone else was being seated. Linus must have seen the effort it took for her to look happy, because he whispered in her ear as he slid the heavy chair smoothly toward the table. "Scott's in surgery. Everything is going to be okay. You're doing great."

They weren't fancy words. But they were the words she needed to hear. Bolstered by his reassurances and the hope that Scott would survive to share what he'd learned, she found the strength to make it, smiling, through the meal without letting on to her sister just how horribly everything in her world was falling apart.

Linus studied the photographs the forensic team had taken of the burned documents Sam had saved. The burned pages themselves were sealed in a box lined with cotton wool, the individual wisps of blackened paper separated by tissue paper, though Linus couldn't imagine they'd be any more legible that way than in the pictures that had been taken before they'd been moved from the hotel room.

Even magnified several times, the printed words were nearly the same color as the burned paper and almost impossible to make out.

But it was all they had to go on. And the fact that the man who'd shot Scott had taken the time to light the papers on fire meant their contents must be important.

Scott Gordon had spent the night in surgery. As of that morning, he had yet to wake up. The last Linus had heard, they didn't know if he would wake up.

Scott had lost a great deal of blood and coded twice on the table, though they'd managed to bring him back both times. Even if he awakened, he might not remember anything of what he'd been going to tell them.

So the pages on the table were their best hope for sorting out what Scott had known. Until they figured that out, they couldn't know why Julia also had been targeted. And until they knew why she'd been targeted, she wouldn't be perfectly safe.

"Knock knock," a female voice chanted from the doorway.

Linus recognized the voice, but he still felt a foolish grin rise to his lips when he turned to see Julia enter, her hair pulled up in a casual ponytail, her T-shirt and shorts reminiscent of what she'd worn the first night he'd saved her, the sneakers on her feet the same that had scuffled in the sand with the footprints of her attacker.

"Come on in." He tried to wipe the grin off his face. When that failed, he looked down at the pages spread on the table, as though he could focus on their contents with Julia standing beside him, smelling fresh and flowery, a bright contrast to the photographs of blackened paper.

She stood in silence for a time, surveying the charred documents before speaking. "Have we learned anything?"

"Scott Gordon wears a size thirteen shoe." He glanced up, and her face held his gaze.

Relief filled her features. "He didn't attack me on the beach that night."

"He didn't." Linus nodded firmly. "But we don't know who did."

"The same guy who shot him?"

Linus had already watched the footage shot by the helicopter's on-board camera. "It's quite possible. The figure appeared to be roughly the same size as Scott. He also had a driver in the car waiting for him. From the brief image the helicopter camera captured when the men ran into the market, the driver was also of similar build. Either of them could have been the man who attacked you on the beach."

"We don't know anything more about them?"

"They're not afraid to shoot." Linus offered her the conclusions he'd reached. "And they don't want anyone to read these papers."

Julia absorbed the news by letting out a long, slow breath, but she didn't break eye contact. "Do you think it's foolish for me to agree to have the titling ceremony on Sunday?"

Linus had been pondering the same question ever since Queen Monica had revealed the plan to her sister. He'd resigned himself to a few conclusions. "From what I can tell, these guys, whoever they might be, are trying to keep a lid on something. They killed Pendleton to keep him quiet. They tried to destroy these papers because they're afraid of what the contents reveal. When Scott resisted their attempts to take him with them, they shot him. I get the sense they're trying to cover up something. If that's the case, they're not going to show their faces at a large public gathering, especially not with all the photographers who will be present."

Julia nodded along as though she agreed with everything he'd said. "They haven't come after me here at the palace yet.

They seem to recognize that the walls and guards and security cameras would make it tough to get to me. They've only ever come after me when I've stepped out."

"The titling ceremony will take place in the throne room, with a reception in the ballroom immediately following. You won't be leaving the palace. The royal guard will be on hand in full force, and Jason has already talked to the Lydian army about providing additional men on site."

"You'd think if these guys wanted to try to reach me inside the palace, they'd avoid showing up on the one day when there's so much extra security."

Linus agreed. "The only advantage I could see from their standpoint would be the added crowd of people. They might hope to blend in with everyone else."

"That's a possibility," Julia acknowledged, planting her hands on the edge of the table as though she needed the added support. "Monica was going to make sure the newspapers carried a notice of increased security along with the announcement of the ceremony. Hopefully that will be enough to deter them."

"The most important thing is that you feel safe." Linus placed a hand on her shoulder.

She let go of the table and looked up at him. It wasn't until she straightened to her full height that he realized how close together they were standing. Her eyes glistened with appreciation as they met his. "You make me feel safe."

Linus couldn't speak. The duchess was so close to him, her face mere inches from his. Her lips hovered so near. It wouldn't take anything at all to kiss her.

"That's—" he struggled to find words and pulled his hand from her shoulder "—that's the most important thing."

"We also need to keep my sister from feeling any additional stress. She tries not to show it, but she's hurting somehow. I can't quite put my finger on it. I don't think it's an emotional toll. She seems quite happy when she's with Thaddeus, and of course with Peter, too. Do you suppose she's ill?"

"It's possible. When she insisted on moving up your titling ceremony, I wondered—" Linus clamped his mouth shut, fearing he'd said too much.

"You wondered what?"

"Just that it almost seems as if she wants to get the titling ceremony over with to make way for something else."

"Something else?"

"I can't say what." Linus immediately felt foolish for even bringing it up, and struggled to make sense of the incoherent sense he'd gotten from the scheduling change. "I just know that the palace administration has gone to great lengths to keep all the events and upcoming royal weddings separate. They're strategic about when they schedule things and when they announce them, so they don't step on anyone's toes."

"You think my sister wants to get my titling ceremony out of the way, so she doesn't step on my toes with an announcement?" Julia's words were soft, not accusational.

"It's possible."

"It's more than possible. It fits. I just hope whatever it is she wants to announce, that it's something good. I hope she's not sick."

Julia gripped the side of the table once more, needing something to lean on. She hated to think that Monica might be ill, but she didn't know how else to explain her sister's pallor or her thinning figure. Monica had always dealt well with stress, so even the stress of becoming queen and moving to Lydia shouldn't have had such a negative effect on her.

An illness was the most logical answer. What hurt Julia even more, though, was that her sister had yet to tell her what it was. Growing up, they'd always shared their secrets.

If Monica had something important to share, she must have a good reason for not wanting to tell Julia. But what was it?

Linus pulled out a chair for her. "Sit. Can I get you anything to drink?"

Julia realized he must have picked up on how unsteady she felt. She sat as instructed and noticed the coffee on warm at the kitchenette in the corner. "I'd take some of that coffee."

"With milk?"

She smiled up at him. "You know how I like it."

Moments later he handed her a steaming cup, and she gripped it, grateful for the warmth that spread up her fingers and the kindness of Linus's gesture. She turned to the enlarged photographs of charred paper spread out on the table before her.

But Linus didn't seem eager to discuss them just yet. "You've been quite concerned about your sister's well-being—even more so than your own, it seems to me."

Julia sipped the warm beverage, then sighed. "I owe it to Monica after all she's been through. Not just the kidnapping earlier this summer, but everything. We never knew she'd snuck off and married Thaddeus six years ago. When we realized she was pregnant, we waited for her to tell us the whole story." Julia studied the swirl of milk that spread into the darker brown of her coffee.

"She never did?" Linus asked gently.

"Never. And instead of pressing for an answer, we just got used to not knowing."

"Don't feel bad. You did what you thought was best."

Julia understood his words, but she couldn't accept them. "Her husband went into hiding for the sake of this kingdom. We should have been there for her, but we didn't know. I thought it was best to give her space, but looking back, I'm afraid I wasn't there for her when she needed me. I regret that. I only wish I knew how to make up for it."

"From what I understand, she couldn't have told you anyway. Thaddeus told her not to tell anyone anything. Doing so would have endangered her and Peter, even you and your parents."

Julia looked up at the handsome guard and studied his face for some time. His expression was earnest, intent. She knew he spoke the truth, but she couldn't shake the guilt she felt. "I still feel as though I should have done something more."

"You can't go back and change the past."

A small smile crept to her lips. "You've said that before, in one way or another."

"It's true," he said, then blew out a frustrated huff of air. "You're not the only one blaming yourself for not stopping the events that happened in June. The whole royal guard has some level of survivor's guilt, Jason worst of all. He thinks he should have been able to stop the ambush and keep the royal family from ever being attacked in the first place."

"But if he'd done that, Thaddeus never would have come out of hiding. Monica wouldn't be queen, and I'd have never been to Lydia. I'd have never met you."

Linus met her eyes again. He opened his mouth, unspoken words on his lips. Then he cleared his throat. "That's true. And I wouldn't have these burnt papers to examine."

Julia welcomed the change of subject. She hadn't meant to bring up her feelings for the guard, knowing as she did that nothing could come of them. "What have you learned from the papers?"

Linus stood and leaned over the images. "The pages that were on the bottom of the pile are copies of newspaper reports. Nearly all of them cover the failures of the engine Pendleton designed."

"The one he tried to sell to Motormech?"

"Precisely. Most of the failures resulted in accidents that caused only injuries. But after a few of those reports came out, Seattle Electronics had two engineers test the SE323 to prove it was safe. Balfour and Chen."

"The two who died when the engine malfunctioned?"

"Exactly. It wasn't safe."

Julia studied the reports, some of which had been burned around the edges, though the bulk of the articles were still legible, and she could fill in the gaps based on what bits were still legible. If she'd thought it important, she could always look up the articles again. But she didn't see how the articles related to the attacks against her, or Pendleton's death.

"Do you suppose someone was upset with Pendleton for designing a faulty engine? Did they kill him for revenge?"

"It's possible," Linus said as he blew out a frustrated breath, "but then why replace the design pages in your file drawer?"

"To cover up their motive?"

"You're right about covering up a motive. They said something to Scott about being a scapegoat. But that still doesn't tell us who pulled the trigger. It doesn't help us keep you safe in the future."

Julia sighed, feeling at a loss. "What about the top pages that suffered the worst burns? It would seem to me Scott would have put the most important evidence at the forefront."

"It's hard to make out any words, but I've spotted *Motormech* a couple of times."

"The company that tried to buy Fletcher's design? But that was two years ago—why would Motormech still be relevant?"

"I've been asking myself that same question. But what did Scott say to you on the phone last night about the break-in at your office? That's when the *Seattle Electronics vs. Pendleton* file was disturbed."

Julia nodded along slowly. "Scott's fingerprints were on that file, and his copy code was used that night." Unable to sit still, Julia rose and paced the room, setting the scene and filling in the gaps as best she could. "Scott was at the office the night of the break-in. Two men came and asked to be let into my office. Scott used the key in Joan's credenza cabinet to let them in. He thought he was helping." She turned in her pacing and looked at Linus to see if he agreed with what she'd worked out so far.

He crossed his arms over his chest and picked up the thread of the story. "They had the altered design pages—the ones that were different from Fletcher's original design." His eyes snapped up and met hers. "The design he emailed you. Your laptop."

"We haven't checked it yet! In all this excitement, I forgot about it. It wasn't in my room last night."

"The guards were supposed to secure it. The guys who were on shift worked late last night with everything that was going on. I'm not sure who's here—"

"It can wait another moment," Julia assured him. "Let's not lose track of Scott's story. The two men wanted to replace the pages in the design file. Furthermore, I can guess why they wanted Scott to make the copies."

"To get his fingerprints all over them, so he could be their scapegoat?" Linus used the same term Scott had given over the phone.

"That too." Julia nodded. "And also so the paper type would match what was in my file folder. They didn't want me to realize what they'd done."

"So they asked Scott to make the copies for them. He thought he was being helpful." Linus repeated the explanation Scott had given.

"But at some point he must have become suspicious, because they threatened him."

"His fingerprints were all over the papers."

"He's a lawyer, he knows how evidence works."

"He was scared." Linus recalled what Scott had said, then

made a conclusive jump forward. "But afterward, he decided to follow up on what these guys were up to. Maybe to cover his own trail if they ever tried to pin anything on him. So he did some searching."

"At some point, they must have realized he was on to them."

"And that's what led them to you," Linus concluded. "They knew they needed to tie up all their loose ends before Scott blew the whistle on them."

Julia felt a cold shiver run up her spine at his words. "But, who are *they?* Why do they care about the engine design in my file cabinet?"

"I think it's time we take a look at your laptop."

"I agree."

Julia followed him down the hall in search of the device, praying desperately that they'd be able to find it, that it would still contain the file…and most importantly, that they'd finally get some answers.

TWELVE

"Please, Lord, please," Julia whispered as she scrolled through a list of old saved files she'd pulled up from the hard drive.

As Linus watched, praying silently along with her, she selected a file to open.

The file must have been large, because it took the computer a few long moments to retrieve it. Julia's hands rose above the keys, balled with tension, and Linus reached over her shoulders to cup her fingers in his.

The computer seemed to freeze up for a moment, and Linus feared they'd crashed it trying to open the bulky document. The computer had to be at least two years old, if Julia had owned it since the time Fletcher had sent her the file. For most things, two years wasn't old. But for computers, two years could be a lifetime. He prayed the machine wasn't dead.

Finally the document opened.

"Yes!" Julia exclaimed gratefully.

Linus freed her fingers and her right hand flew to the mouse pad, dragging down through the document to the pages that had been replaced in her file.

"There it is—there it is!" She nearly squealed with relief as she jumped out of her chair.

Linus wasn't quite ready for her sudden action. He started to jump back, but she already had her arms around him.

"It's Fletcher's file." She held him in a tight celebratory hug.

Linus held her to him, so relieved at the break in the case that he didn't immediately peel himself away.

That, and he didn't want to be anywhere else but close to her.

A moment later, Julia pulled back. Though she turned her attention immediately to the computer, Linus could see the blush that colored her cheeks. "Sorry," she whispered, glancing at the closed door behind them, "I know I'm not supposed to—"

"It's okay." He squeezed her hand and nodded toward the image that filled the screen. "It's different from the one in your file, isn't it? It's subtle, but it's different." Linus was no automotive expert, but he'd stared at the pages from Julia's file long enough to spot a few changes.

"Yes, I think you're right. Can we print this? I don't want to lose it."

Linus helped her connect her laptop to a printer. While several copies of the document churned out, they backed up the document and emailed a copy to themselves and Jason. Holding the printed pages, Linus felt the lingering hand of doubt suppress his relief that they'd retrieved the evidence. "Julia?"

"Yes?" She held another copy and paged through it, still clearly marveling that she finally held the important pages in her hands.

He hated to burst her bubble, but the question needed to be asked. "What does it mean?"

Her expression fell slightly. "I don't know, but someone went to an awful lot of trouble to make these pages disappear. It has to be something important. It was worth killing over."

* * *

Since Julia had originally come to Lydia for the express purpose of spending time with her sister, she knew she ought to do so when she had the chance that afternoon, even if she felt a burning desire to study the photographs of the burnt documents laid out on the conference room table at the royal guard headquarters. She was nearly certain Linus would be there, though she was equally sure he was supposed to be off duty after all the overtime he'd put in on her behalf. But he'd intimated that he had no intention of letting the investigation go on without him, not as long as Julia's attackers remained at large.

The thought warmed her, though she also felt a twinge of guilt. The warring emotions kept her distracted as Monica discussed the plans for the titling ceremony.

"Would you prefer a cake, cupcake tower or cake pop display?"

"Hmm?"

"Yoo-hoo." Monica waved her hand in front of Julia's line of sight, and giggled. "I'm over here, planning your reception. Where are you?"

Julia got her mouth open, but couldn't force any words out.

"You'll have a full royal guard escort," Monica continued. "Would you prefer to see Linus in a bow tie or ascot?"

Julia stared at her sister and blinked.

Monica laughed. "I thought that would get your attention."

"I, uh..." Julia cleared her throat and tried in vain not to blush. "Linus?"

"Yes." Monica's eyes danced with amusement. "That guard you keep hoping to see every time you hear footsteps enter the room."

Footsteps sounded on the parquet wood floors behind them, and Julia turned to look, half-certain it *would* be Linus this time, and fearing he'd overheard Monica's teasing.

But it was only King Thaddeus with Prince Peter on his shoulders. "We're off to the dedication of the new playground," Thaddeus announced, blowing his wife a kiss.

"Have fun, darlings." Monica blew a kiss back, and the king stepped out again, with Peter blowing kisses behind them.

"Are you sure you don't want to go with them?" Julia asked hesitantly. She enjoyed spending time with her sister, but she'd have welcomed an excuse to end the queen's line of questions.

"No. I want to spend time with you."

Julia realized with a pang why they couldn't *both* go along to the playground dedication. They'd already determined that the safest place for her was within the palace walls. They didn't want to risk another attack—and a playground dedication was no place for an encounter with the desperate men who'd killed Fletcher and shot Scott.

"Julia?" Monica's expression sobered at her sister's extended silence. "I didn't mean to hurt your feelings. Maybe I shouldn't have teased, but I need to know if you want Linus to serve as your escort for the event. Given the circumstances, it makes sense to have a member of the royal guard beside you at all times, and what better place for him than on your arm? But if you don't want Linus—"

"Of course I want Linus." Julia clamped her mouth shut after she'd said it, unsure if she should have spoken, but unwilling to make her sister babble on and on. She wished Monica would go back to her teasing—the serious tone was worse. Julia would have preferred that her sister not pick up on her feelings for Linus, especially when she herself had yet to sort out what those feelings were.

But Monica's brow only furrowed deeper. "It's more than just a silly crush, then, is it? He hasn't hurt your feelings—"

"Of course not!" Julia protested, perhaps a little too adamantly. She tried to sound casual. "Linus has only ever been a gentleman. He's been perfectly...perfect." Julia wished she could think of a way to assure her sister that Linus was an excellent guard, in spite of whatever they might later learn of his juvenile criminal record. But how could she do that without bringing up the very record she wished to keep hidden?

Monica continued to probe for details. "You *do* like him?"

"Is it that obvious?"

Monica nodded.

Julia wondered if Jason or the other guards had caught on to anything. She couldn't let Linus risk a review, not with everything else going on. "It doesn't matter anyway. I shouldn't even be thinking about such things until this whole matter with my attacker is resolved."

Monica nodded solemnly and let the subject drop. "What do you think of cake pops? Too trendy?"

Her abrupt willingness to end the discussion aroused Julia's suspicions. "You're not going to say anything to Linus, are you?"

"Julia..." Monica placed a hand over her heart as though she'd been insulted. "Of course I'm not going to speak to *Linus*. I just needed to find out if you want him as your escort on Sunday."

"I don't know if I do."

"Of course you do. Now let's just talk about the cake."

Linus used a magnifying glass to inspect the photographic images of the burned pages, making notes of any words or parts of words he could pick out. His notes looked like a mess of random letters. *Squigg. Envirotek. EEGS.* They weren't even real words.

He couldn't make heads or tails of any of it. But neither could he give up.

Jason cleared his throat from the doorway. It was an ominous throat clearing, the kind that usually preceded a lecture.

Linus had known his supervisor long enough to interpret the sound before he'd even laid eyes on him.

One look at Jason's face confirmed it.

"What did I do?" Linus lowered the magnifying glass.

"For one, you don't seem to understand the words *off duty*. It's seven in the evening and you haven't had dinner yet. You weren't even scheduled to work today."

"*You're* still here."

That edged a smile to Jason's lips, but he cleared his throat again, and Linus knew that hadn't been the subject the head of the guard had come to lecture him about.

"I spoke with their majesties the king and queen. They're worried about Julia."

"I'm doing everything I can—"

"That's why they're worried. More specifically, I believe Queen Monica is concerned about the nature of your attention to her little sister."

Linus felt his ears flame red. "I haven't—I haven't done anything or said anything." He'd specifically kept his emotions in check, even when it had been quite difficult to do so. What could the queen possibly have seen?

Jason rubbed his hands across his face. He was only a few years older than Linus, but the burden of running the royal guard in such trying times had already begun to show its toll. "This isn't a good time for this. The fact is, Linus, Queen Monica would like to request you to be Julia's personal escort for the titling ceremony."

"I'd be honored."

"But she needs to know that her sister…" He rubbed his face again and made a grunt of frustration. "If I may speak plainly—"

"I wish you would." Linus met Jason's eyes and might have laughed if his old friend hadn't been acting so frighteningly serious.

"I know you're an honorable member of the royal guard, but we have standards to uphold. You know your record. I wish I could erase history, but if you come up for review, it will also have to come out. I can't set a double standard for my friends."

"Are you worried that there might be something between me and Julia?"

"Worried?" Jason shook his head somberly. "You've been my friend far too long to try to hide. I've seen the two of you together. I know there's something going on. The queen suspects it, as well. Just promise me one thing, if you can."

"Yes?"

"Don't cross the line with the duchess. If you get caught, you'll be subject to immediate review. Understood?"

"Completely."

"Excellent." Jason smiled. "Then you can come with me now. The duchess has received a large envelope via international mail. I've asked Sam to bring her to the conference room to open it."

Linus straightened. "Any ID on the sender?"

"The return address indicates one Fletcher Pendleton."

"You know he was murdered, right?" Linus had filled his boss in on all those details, but it wouldn't have surprised him if, with everything else that had been going on, the name had slipped his mind.

"Before his death, Fletcher told Julia to expect a package, correct?" Jason entered the conference room and stepped to the side as Linus followed him in.

"That's right." Linus spotted the package on the table, with Oliver hovering warily nearby, almost as though they feared the envelope might be stolen if it was left unguarded. "So this is the package he sent her?"

"Oh, my!"

Linus turned in time to see Julia enter the room, her fingers covering her mouth. She looked warily at the envelope as though it might hurt her.

She glanced up at him, then back at the parcel. "He really *did* send me a package."

"He did," Linus confirmed, wishing he could wrap her in his arms and comfort her, but he'd just promised Jason he'd do nothing of the sort.

"I suppose I should open it."

"When you're ready."

Though the package on the table frightened her, Julia took comfort knowing that Linus was there, even if he wasn't technically on duty. She approached the package cautiously and tried not to think about the fate of its sender.

Linus helped her peel back the seal, peeking inside when they had it halfway open. "It just looks like a bunch of papers." His tone bore a mixture of relief and disappointment.

"Hopefully the papers will give us some answers." The adhesive loosened its grip under her steady hand, and a moment later the envelope gaped open.

"Careful now." Linus spread out his hands to catch the contents as Julia tipped the envelope toward him. A sheaf of papers slid out neatly, and he caught them.

The top page was a cover letter on Fletcher Pendleton's personal stationery, dated August 14, the same day Julia had arrived in Lydia the first time. The same day—or within twenty-four hours—of the break-in at her house.

She took a tiny gulp and turned the paper to read, standing back from the table so the guards could see everything she saw. She read quickly, unable to absorb every word in her haste to sort out the meaning. Certain lines stood out far more starkly than others.

It is imperative that someone know the truth… No one from Seattle Electronics will talk to me… As you know, Seattle Electronics was awarded all my work on the engine I designed for them. At the time, I felt guilty for my involvement. I gave them every scrap of paper, every file, every sketch of the design I had created.

I saw the headlines about the malfunctions with the SE323… I realized something was wrong. I convinced one of my key associates from Seattle Electronics to pass along to me the current design. Though mostly unchanged from my memories of the original engine, it contained a few minor but horrifying alterations.

The engine I designed was safe. It would not have malfunctioned…

I no longer have the documents detailing my original design, but I have recreated them from memory and highlighted the differences for you.

Scour your files for some evidence of my original design… These changes may have caused the accidents, including the one that killed Balfour and Chen.

Julia felt a chill run through her as she read the letter. She'd have found Pendleton's words alarming enough if she'd read the words a week before. Now that Fletcher was dead—murdered—the words hit her like blows to the stomach.

She studied them for several long minutes even after she'd first read through the letter.

"Oh," she moaned and clutched at the base of her throat, trying not to let her stomach lurch, though her thoughts spun with sickening madness.

Why would Seattle Electronics sabotage their own design? Balfour and Chen were the engineers who'd died trying to prove the engine was safe. Why would their engineers test a prototype they'd knowingly tampered with? Had Balfour and Chen committed suicide?

Or had they been murdered, too?

Along with the other guards looking over her shoulders, Linus had studied the letter for several long minutes. He now looked up at her with a face drained of color beneath his Mediterranean tan. "He says he's included the original engine design." His bass voice fell even deeper than usual, a hollow whisper filled with dread.

Julia wished she could pinch her eyes shut against the truth, but still she flipped through the pages Pendleton had sent her, hoping against hope that the changed portions of the design weren't the same as those that had been replaced in her file.

But of course they were. She'd studied them too closely in the last day not to recognize them immediately. The copy Pendleton had provided her with, which he'd obtained from a Seattle Electronics associate, looked identical to the pages that had been replaced in her file.

Jason must have realized what they were both thinking. "The printouts you two made of the design from Julia's file," he said, then looked at Sam. "Bring those in for a side-by-side comparison. Also grab the copies of the fingerprinted pages from Julia's file cabinet."

While Sam ran down the hall to fetch the requested documents, Julia laid out the pages in a line—one row of Fletcher's recreated original, the other row of the altered design Seattle Electronics had sent to production. Sam returned with the pages she'd printed out. She arranged them above the others.

She was no engineer, but with the help of Fletcher's highlighted alterations, she was quickly able to match one design to the other. The only trick was figuring out why the switch had been made, and how it connected to the attack against Scott, the attack against her and Fletcher's murder.

"The design Fletcher emailed me two years ago matches his recreated design," she recounted. "Seattle Electronics altered that design before they sent it into production. And then—" Her voice faltered as she reached for the copied pages that still bore Scott's dusted fingerprints.

Linus picked up her line of thought. "Someone broke into your office and replaced the original design with the altered design. They wanted it to look like the design that caused the accident had been the real design all along."

"But why bother?" Oliver shook his head as he scowled at the pages. "She wasn't going to look at the pages again. They were filed away and forgotten. Why stir things up?"

"Fletcher was asking questions," Julia said as she picked up the cover letter included in the package. "He had someone from Seattle Electronics forward him the production design. Who knows who else he talked to and who overheard? Whoever made this change didn't want anyone to know about it— that's when they decided to cover their tracks."

Linus nodded. "That's when Fletcher started calling you, wanting to meet."

"He wanted his original design. I just thought he was acting creepy."

"He may have been acting creepy precisely because he suspected these guys were on to him," Linus concluded.

"And he was right," Julia said with a sigh, "but who are *they?* What did they have to gain by making the design worse instead of better?"

"Maybe they thought they were making it better?" Sam suggested halfheartedly.

Oliver, the tech expert among them, shook his head. "It seems doubtful. In his letter, Fletcher called them horrifying alterations. Surely other engineers would recognize the danger."

"Chen and Balfour," Linus repeated the names of the engineers who'd died testing the SE323. "I read the newspaper articles about the crash—the reports Scott tried to give to Julia. Basically any time the car went over 75 mph, it overheated and crashed. The occupants were either injured or killed."

Julia tried to put the pieces together. "Pendleton's original design was altered before it went into production as the SE323. It seems he believed the malfunctions that caused injuries and, ultimately, the deaths of the Balfour and Chen, wouldn't have happened if Seattle Electronics had stuck to his original design."

Jason sounded disgusted. "So why did they change it? And why did Balfour and Chen test the model themselves when they already knew it had problems? Isn't that what crash test dummies are for?"

Julia couldn't help feeling suspicious. "You'd think they'd know better."

"I don't recall ever seeing the engineers' credentials," Linus mused. "Perhaps we should look into it."

Oliver stood. "I'm on it."

Linus grinned appreciatively. "See what you can learn about the crash that killed Balfour and Chen. There were other incidents, too. Learn whatever you can about those accidents. We still don't know how this connects to Scott or to Julia, really."

"Where there's murder, there must be motive," Oliver quipped.

"Yeah," Linus agreed sullenly. "And Julia's not going to be safe until we figure out what that motive was." He met her eyes.

In spite of the warning in his words, she saw reassurance there. He was watching out for her. He was determined to protect her. She just hoped that would be enough.

THIRTEEN

"I had an idea last night." Monica burst into Julia's room bright and early the next morning. "I couldn't sleep until Thaddeus gave me a map."

"It's a treasure map!" Five-year-old Peter followed his mother into Julia's bedroom and flung himself onto her bed, leaping excitedly. "It's how we found my mom when Octoman had her!"

"Peter, please remember your manners. We do not jump on beds." She addressed her son in a firm tone, then turned to Julia, who'd been reading her Bible in the window seat. "It's not a treasure map. It's a map of the secret passages in the palace. And those *did* come in handy when Octavian wanted to kill me. That's what gave me the idea." Monica spread out a large roll of paper on the bedside desk.

"Secret passages?" Julia felt intrigued, but she wasn't sure she understood her sister's plans. She closed her Bible and stood beside her sister as she looked at the hand-drawn map. "What are you thinking?"

"I know the guards keep saying your attackers won't come after you inside the palace, but what if they do?"

"You don't need to *worry*," Julia rushed to assure her sister.

"I won't worry if I know that you know how to find your

way through all the secret passages. That way, if anything happens, you'll have a means of escape."

Julia tried to absorb the intricacies of the maze of passages. "How am I supposed to learn them all? I hardly know my way around the not-so-secret parts of the palace."

"You can learn them by walking them. You have three days."

"So you're planning to drag me through all these passages yourself?"

"No. I have an appointment this morning, and other things on my schedule later today. But Linus can explore them with you. He'll be your escort Sunday, so he's the most likely person to be with you if you need to duck through a wall or—look at this one—around a rotating bookshelf. Isn't that clever?"

"Clever," Julia repeated, already thinking about seeing Linus again, and her sister's convenient plan to shove them together for the morning. "Very clever."

Julia spotted Linus as he entered through the back gate, casually dressed in cargo shorts and a blue-and-red plaid madras shirt. She met him before he reached the royal guard headquarters.

"What are your plans today?" she asked breathlessly, the map rolled up like a baton in her hand.

Linus looked slightly sheepish. "I'm supposed to have the day off—"

"Oh." She took a step back, instantly feeling guilty that she'd bothered him during his personal time. "Don't let me interrupt you."

"I was going to take another look at the burned documents today. I couldn't fall asleep last night, trying to figure out what they meant."

Julia realized Linus looked tired. She wanted to smooth away every trace of exhaustion from his eyes.

"Did you need help with something?" Linus glanced from the map in her hand back to her face.

Julia realized she'd been looking overly long at his warm brown eyes. Instead she turned her attention to the map rolled up in her hand. "Oh, it's not anything that important. Just an idea Monica had—"

"What is it?" Linus lowered the bag he was toting onto the cobblestones.

"I don't want to bother you on your day off—"

"I'm already bothered."

"But you've already done so much—"

"I haven't done enough. You're not safe yet."

"I don't want to trouble you."

"It's no trouble. What's worse? For me to work with you on whatever idea Monica had, or for me to stare at those burned papers until I go crazy trying to figure them out?"

"You're sure you don't just want to go fishing like a normal day off?"

"I'm not that much into fishing, actually."

Julia realized she didn't know what Linus did with his spare time. She'd never known him to have any. He'd only ever been at her side. "Hunting, then?"

"I don't like to shoot things—not unless they're threatening me or someone I care about."

Whether it was the meaning of his words or the tenderness in his eyes when he spoke them, Julia felt a ripple of affection as he spoke. "Hiking?"

"Hiking." He nodded. "I like to hike. But not today. I'd only be worried about how you were faring in my absence."

Julia liked to hike, too. And she'd never been keen on fishing or hunting. The similarity in their interests made her smile. Distracted, she hardly noticed Linus reaching for the map until he had one hand cupped over hers.

"Is this what Monica gave you?"

She couldn't lie to him. "Yes, actually, but I don't want to keep you from anything important."

"There's nothing more important than your safety." He'd gotten the map from her and spread it wide, a grin forming on his face as he recognized it for what it was. His eyes sparkled when he turned to her again. "I've heard of this, but I've never had clearance to look at a copy. Only royals are allowed to know the secrets of the palace."

"My sister got it from King Thaddeus," Julia said, instantly feeling guilty for being given something so precious when she didn't really deserve it.

"You're royal." Linus seemed to sense her hesitation. "You have every right to it."

"Not technically, not until Sunday."

He exhaled impatiently, as though implying that her protests were as unsubstantial as the air around them. "What's the plan, then?"

"Monica thinks we should explore the secret passages. If we're familiar with them, we can use them to escape or hide if anyone comes after me within the palace walls."

Linus let the map roll back with the snap. "I've always wanted to explore the secret passages of the palace. And you thought I'd rather go fishing? Let me stash my bag in my locker and we can get started."

Linus pulled open the drawer were he kept extra high-powered flashlights. They'd surely need an alternate light source in the secret passages, some of which were tunnels that ran between walls, up and down various levels of floors, and underground. There were even rumors about tunnels that connected with the catacombs of Charlemagne that ran beneath the city, though those were all supposed to have been filled in years ago.

His grandfather, who'd been a member of the royal guard during World War II, had told tales of sneaking the royal family out under the cover of darkness to escape threats from Nazi double agents. Part of the reason Linus had become a royal guard was because he'd always enjoyed his grandfather's stories. As a child, he'd imagined what it might be like to explore those ancient corridors.

He'd never dreamed he'd get to do so with a beautiful duchess at his side.

But even as he gripped his flashlight and turned to face the lovely lady waiting in his doorway, Linus knew the task before him was far more serious than any enjoyable exploration he might have dreamed about as a child. "Ready?"

Julia grinned at him, sending his heart into a dizzy dance. "I'm looking forward to it. I've always wanted to explore the palace—the secret passages are like an added bonus. This may be the most fun I've had in Lydia."

Recalling how her jog on the beach had gone, Linus couldn't help agreeing with her. "Where do you want to start?" He spread out the map on his desk and studied the mazelike layout.

"Anywhere." She stood beside him to look at the large map.

Linus nearly cut off her words as he sucked in an excited breath.

"What is it?" Julia asked, leaning closer.

With his elbow holding the map flat against its preconditioned roll, Linus pointed to hand-lettered markings. "Executioner's Escape," he read aloud, the two words transporting him back in time to the stories his grandfather had told him years before.

"Executioner?" Julia repeated. "Was capital punishment practiced on the Lydian palace grounds?"

Linus closed his eyes and tried to remember. His grand-father's stories had focused on the events of seventy years before, not seven hundred. And yet, he'd asked that same question of his grandfather once. He tried to recall the answer.

"The royal family of Lydia didn't always live in the palace in Sardis. For many hundreds of years they lived in a castle at the end of a peninsula that extended beyond the mainland. But centuries of storms have washed away the land, leaving the archipelago of islands we have now. The ruins of the first Lydian royal castle are on what's now called the Island of Dorsi."

Julia listened in rapt attention, her eyes aglow as he re-counted the changes that had taken place in Lydia's storied history.

"I can't remember when it was, precisely," Linus said, "but there came a time, I think several hundred years ago, when the kingdom of Lydia was under assault from her enemies. This palace was under construction. It would have been out-side the walls of the city of Sardis, then. When Lydia's en-emies attacked, they took possession of this palace. They planned to execute their Lydian war prisoners in the central courtyard, but they feared the Lydians would try to rescue the prisoners at the last minute, so they built an escape pas-sage for the executioner."

Julia's eyes were wide. "What happened?"

"The people of Lydia came to the aid of their prisoners. It seems to me they rushed into the passage after the execu-tioner, but I'm not sure exactly what happened after that. Any-way, it turned the tide of battle, and Lydia took back these surrounding lands."

Julia blinked down at the words on the map. "It's not clear where the tunnel goes. The map doesn't show the different levels, but it seems there are stairs connecting through that wall."

Linus smiled. That was the part of the story he was most

familiar with. "It's a spiral staircase. It goes up and down from that point. My grandfather's been inside it. I always wanted to explore it myself."

"Then that's where we'll start," Julia said as she beamed up at him. "And you can tell me the story of why your grandfather was inside it—if you don't mind."

"I don't mind at all." Linus carried the map and the flashlights as he led her across the rear courtyard, past the west gardens with their arched arbors canopied with climbing roses, and beyond them, a graceful fountain and picturesque maze of hedges. They ducked through a wide rose-covered archway and entered the interior palace courtyard, a massive, mostly enclosed space surrounded by three levels of continuous balconies, all rimmed with stone balustrades and topped with columns and arches. Above those, smaller balconies jutted out here and there, some with stone stairs winding downward for access from below.

Linus spread the map wide and held it out until it aligned with the architectural masterpiece before him.

Julia held on to his arm near his elbow as she peered at the map, glancing back-and-forth before pointing to a second-floor archway ahead of them. "There," she whispered, as though speaking in a louder voice might somehow give away their plans.

The moment she pointed to the spot, Linus recognized it. Instead of wide windows lined up in orderly rows, the alcove sheltered only a blank stone wall. The arch above it matched all the others, and so masked the significance of the paneless spot.

Rolling up the map again, Linus led the way to the stone steps that curved upward along one interior corner of the courtyard. His heart beat with excitement as he approached the stone wall.

"Now what?" Julia asked, placing her hands almost reverently against the solid stones.

"I'm not sure. The map didn't say how to get through, only that there is a passage beyond." He thought back to the story his grandfather had told him all those years before. The hidden door was designed to swing outward—that detail had been important, because the open door itself had blocked the way of those pursuing his grandfather and the royals, and they'd pulled it shut behind them quickly to cut off anyone who might try to follow them as they escaped.

"There's got to be a handle of some sort to pull on. It can't be very complicated to operate." He ran his hands along the stones, their rough surfaces protruding from the ancient mortar, in some places by several inches.

"Here." Julia slipped her fingers over and behind the jutting face of a stone.

He clasped his hand over hers and they pulled back together. With the sound of grating rocks, the door shifted from its long held jamb and swung out toward them. The momentum of their tug sent the heavy stones swinging with force, and Linus scooped one hand around Julia's waist as he pulled her to the side, out of the way of the swinging door.

Slowly, the pivoting portal ground to a stop, revealing a shadowy space beyond. With the balcony above them blocking much of the sun's rays, there was little to light anything beyond the door. Linus flicked on a flashlight and illuminated the forgotten space, its interior filigreed with drooping spider webs. The dust stirred up by the opening door danced in motes along the beam of his flashlight, veiling what lay beyond.

The duchess linked her fingers with his. "Ready?" she asked in a voice that was half eagerness, half uncertainty.

"I think so." They stepped inside the cool stone-enclosed

space. A few paces ahead, Linus could see stone stairs winding upward, and more steps twisting downward the other way.

"Should we leave the door open behind us?" Julia's question carried a tremor of apprehension, as though she feared they might seal themselves inside the tomblike space.

Normally Linus would have agreed with her, but he knew the passages were to be kept a secret. Julia's own safety might well depend on it within just a few days' time. It wouldn't do to leave the entrance gaping open, exposed for anyone in the household to see. "We need to close it behind us so it stays a secret." He reached past her to pull the heavy stonework toward them.

"Wait." Julia's hands landed on his shoulder and arm. "Are you sure we won't seal ourselves in?"

She was suddenly so very close, looking up at him through the settling dust and lone beam of light, her expression a mixture of trust and uncertainty. Linus realized what a very great gift she'd given him, entrusting herself to him as they explored the long-forgotten corridor together. Rather than allow her to continue to be afraid, he assured her gently, "I know where these stairs lead."

"But how can you? I couldn't tell from the map."

"My grandfather's story," he reminded her.

Her face relaxed. "That's right. I suppose he told you how he got out." She pulled her hands away and tucked them penitently behind her back. "Maybe you should tell me the whole story before I let my fear get the best of me."

"Good idea." Linus pulled the stone door closed, and it settled into place behind them with a solid thud that reverberated through him ominously.

Julia shuffled closer to him again, sharing his tiny alcove of light in the beam of the torch he carried.

He was glad to have her close. The corridor was chilly, and her presence provided warmth, as well as the fresh floral scent that had become so familiar to him over the course of the time he'd spent at her side. Jason had warned him not to get too close to Julia, but here in the long forgotten stone passageways, no one would see if he held her close.

She snuggled against him, away from the chill of the dark space around them.

It would be okay. He wasn't going to cross any lines. He just wouldn't shove her away, either. Settling his hand at her waist again to guide her as they stepped cautiously forward, he began the tale his grandfather had recounted many times.

She listened until he paused at the steps. "Up or down?" she asked.

"Either. My grandfather went up, of course, but we could go either way."

"Up is good. Down sounds like it would involve more darkness. Up should eventually lead us into the light."

He picked up his story as they made their way up the long flight.

She interrupted him again when they paused at a landing that seemed to serve no purpose at all. "We must be on the level of the third floor," she surmised. "But there doesn't seem to be a door."

Linus had already recounted how his grandfather had escaped with the royal family through the hatch to the roof. His story didn't offer them any knowledge of the third floor. "It would make sense for there to be a door—there's a landing," he said, then pressed against the blank stones of the wall.

Julia joined him, both of them slapping their palms against the wall until suddenly the facade gave way and they stood in a narrow room even more cobwebbed than the last. With a shake of her head, Julia tried to blow away the cobwebs that clung to her face and hair.

Linus brushed them away with a swipe of his hands. "You're right—" he laughed "—there *is* a door."

"But where does it lead?" she said as she stepped forward, apparently unaware of how close they already stood to one another.

With his arms still poised in midair from brushing the cobwebs from her face, Linus settled his arms around her almost instinctively. For a moment, she snuggled against him as though that was where she'd wanted to be all along.

He brushed her face with his hand, cupping her chin, wanting to kiss her, but knowing he shouldn't.

She rose up on her tiptoes until her nose brushed his cheek. "Julia?"

"Yes?" The word was soft, almost a sigh of contentment, and he realized he'd wrapped his arms around her so securely, she must feel safe there—safer than she'd felt since before the attack.

"I'm not supposed to get close to you."

She backed away half an inch. "I'm sorry." She sounded embarrassed, even ashamed.

He couldn't stand it. He found her lips in the darkness, kissing her lightly, hesitantly, intending it to be a reassuring kiss that communicated his affection without crossing whatever line it was he wasn't supposed to cross.

Her grip tightened on his sleeves, pulling him close, keeping him near. She kissed him back, surprising him with the unexpected thrill of her touch. He couldn't pull away, but held her closer, letting the kiss grow between them.

The faint vibration in his pocket hardly registered until the phone he'd stashed there began to ring.

"Your phone!" If Julia hadn't heard it, he might not have noticed yet.

He left a tiny kiss on her bottom lip as he pulled back just far enough to check the screen.

"It's Jason." Linus realized his superior officer wouldn't be calling unless it was important—not after the lecture he'd given him the evening before about working on his time off. He answered it quickly.

"The duchess is missing," Jason reported without preamble.

"She's with me," Linus confessed.

"In a secure location?"

"Yes."

"Thank God." Jason's words rose in a grateful prayer, his relief tangible in spite of their less-than-optimum phone connection. "Someone breached our security. We didn't even know he was inside until Galen spotted a dark figure making his escape over the palace wall. The man was long gone by the time our men reached the spot, but they found footprints that matched the cast we took at the beach."

"So it was the same man?"

"Most likely."

"And he climbed over the wall to escape?"

"That must be how he got in, too. I don't know if he accomplished his objective. We're checking our footage to see if we can find where he went."

"Do you want me to help you search?"

"No. Just keep the duchess safe. I've got a phone call to make, then I'll call you again. Whatever you do, don't let the duchess out of your sight. It seems—" Jason swallowed hard enough that Linus could hear it over the phone "—she's not even safe inside the palace."

FOURTEEN

Julia gripped Linus's shoulders and strained to hear Jason's words over the phone. Between the way Linus had tensed up at his supervising officer's words, and the bits she was able to deduce from what Linus said in response, she gathered that something had happened. Something bad, involving her.

"What is it?" she asked when he ended the call.

His arms tightened around her. Grateful as she was for his embrace, she felt too distressed to enjoy it.

"The perimeter," he began, his bass voice carrying an apology, as though the guard felt he'd failed her. "It's been breached."

Julia pressed her face against Linus's shoulder and pinched her eyes shut to hold back the tears that sprang up as the meaning of his words sank in. "Do they think I'm the target?"

"The guards found footprints where he went over the wall on his way out. The prints matched the casting they took at the beach."

"So he's gone."

"Long gone. But they don't know yet why he broke in, or where he went while he was here."

Julia couldn't stand it. Her only relief from her attacker's relentless pursuit had been the safety of the palace walls and the protection of the royal guard. But now it seemed it wasn't enough. "Why wasn't he caught on his way in?"

"There aren't enough screens in the video surveillance room to show every camera at every moment. They rotate through on a regular schedule unless particular screens are selected manually." Linus shook his head regretfully. "The royal guard doesn't have the manpower to monitor every corner of the palace grounds at every moment."

"Not even after all that happened earlier this summer?"

"That's precisely it. Certain members of the royal guard were part of the conspiracy against the royal family. We've had to slash our force, keeping only those men we knew we could trust. We've been hiring new men, but training them takes time, and Jason has been quite particular about only hiring men who are faithful to the crown."

"He might want to be a little less particular, if there aren't enough men to do the job." Julia heard the note of frustration enter her voice, but she couldn't help it. She felt her enemies getting closer, and she still didn't even know who they were.

"It's because there aren't enough men that he hasn't shared what he learned about my record."

Julia softened at that reminder. "I'm glad he's keeping you around. I don't know how I'd manage without you." She held on to Linus, and he pulled her close again. As she nuzzled against him, another thought occurred to her. "Did Jason say whether they'd checked my suite? If the intruder was the same man who came after me before, he may have been headed that way."

"Jason didn't mention it. Shall we take a look?"

Julia closed her eyes and sighed.

Linus brushed his lips across her forehead tenderly. "You ready?"

She didn't want to go. She'd much rather explore the hidden corridors and the feelings she had for Linus. But her enemies wouldn't give her a rest, so she relented to going back out the way they'd come in. "Lead the way."

Linus was glad Julia had told him to lead the way. He had every intention of going in her room first. Just because one man had exited over the wall, that didn't mean he hadn't left an accomplice behind.

When they reached Julia's suite the door was open.

"I'm going to make sure it's clear." Linus hurried ahead.

As he stepped inside, he heard Julia gasp behind him.

She'd obviously seen the mess. Her room had been ransacked just as her home in Seattle had been. It looked like the same handiwork, even.

A couple of royal guards stood near the window, already dusting it for prints. They must have discovered the room while looking for Julia.

Linus stepped closer to the spot where they worked. One balcony window had been jimmied open from outside.

"It's clear," Linus assured Julia.

She had one hand to her mouth as she stepped gingerly over a shattered flower vase before picking her way across the strewn disarray from the toppled parlor set. "I was just in my suite a couple of hours ago—with Monica and little Peter." The thought of what might have happened if her attacker had broken in then, with her sister and five-year-old nephew present, sent a shiver rippling through her.

Linus rested a hand on her shoulder, but when she turned toward him, looking as though she might bury her face against his shoulder, he gave his head a warning shake. The guards were focused on their investigation, but they were still in the room.

"Have you reported to Jason yet?" Linus asked.

"We just arrived shortly before you did," one guard explained. "Feel free to let him know."

Since he was technically off duty and wasn't wearing an earpiece, Linus used his phone to call Jason. The head of the guard sounded disgusted by the news, but not particularly surprised.

"I'll be right over."

True to his word, Jason arrived within minutes. Linus consulted with him in the doorway as Julia roved through the room, her hands clutched around her upper arms, comforting herself. Much as Linus wished to walk along beside her, supporting her, he'd promised Jason he wouldn't cross the line with the duchess. And while he wasn't sure where Jason would draw that line, Linus wasn't about to risk being put out of service now—not when Julia needed him more than ever.

Besides that, Jason had news for him. "The phone call I just made was to Scott Gordon's mother. We're flying her to Lydia. The doctors have told me the best we can hope for at this point is that she arrives in time to sign a release for organ donation."

"There's no hope, then?"

"Not for Scott, not in this life." Jason shook his head regretfully.

Linus met Julia's eyes from across the room. He knew she couldn't have heard Jason's muted words, not with the ocean breeze pouring in through the broken window. But she'd have to learn what was up sooner or later. He tried to muster an encouraging smile. She looked as if she needed it.

"They've gone through the contents of my suitcase," she reported as she approached them, "but nothing of mine appears to be missing."

"Your laptop is still at the royal guard headquarters," Linus said for Jason's benefit.

"That must be what they were after," Julia said, then blew out a tension-filled breath. "If they're determined to get it, I suppose—" she met his eyes with a look that was nine-tenths terror, one-tenth steely determination "—they'll try to go through me to get it."

"They're after the design file?" Jason asked. "Have we ever figured out why that's significant?"

"We know the design was altered so that the engine malfunctions over speeds of 75 miles per hour," Julia explained, "but we've never figured out who made the decision to change it, or what their motive possibly could have been."

"Oliver was researching Balfour and Chen," Jason noted. "Touch base with him and find out what he's learned."

"Good idea," Linus agreed, as much to give the duchess something to focus on as anything. He didn't expect the dead men to provide them with any more clues than Scott could.

Jason took a step toward the door. "Just stay clear of the conference room. Simon's overseeing the installation of more security screens, and the conference room has the most available wall space. We want to be able to monitor the views from as many of the security cameras as possible, but we need to have the system installed and tested by Sunday."

Linus was glad to hear the plan, and immediately latched onto a possibility it presented—and an answer to a problem that had nagged at him since he'd learned that Julia's attacker had breached the palace wall. He tapped Jason on the shoulder with the rolled map he still held, stopping his supervisor before he left. "I have something."

"What's that?" Jason looked at the map as Linus unrolled it, spreading it flat against the mattress that rested askew atop the box spring.

"A very confidential document." Linus held one end while Julia flatted the other to prevent the map from rolling back on itself.

"The secret corridors!" Jason exclaimed as he bent over the parchment. "I need a copy of this."

"You'll need the king's permission," Linus reminded him,

"but I agree—if we can keep it classified, with only the most trusted men allowed to lay eyes on it, the royal guard should have access to this information. More than that, I think we need to position our security cameras to view the entrances and exits to the passages."

Jason's eyes showed hope for the first time that morning. "If the attackers breach the walls again, the duchess can take cover in the passages."

"And if I'm with her, getting transmissions via earpiece from the men watching the security footage, they can tell me when it's safe to come and go."

"It gives us an advantage. We can stay one step ahead of them." Jason's lips bent into a firm smile. "We can proceed with the titling ceremony as planned."

Julia helped Linus move the burnt document photos to a smaller room away from the wires and workmen that filled the conference room as they transformed the space into a state-of-the-art surveillance center. They found Oliver helping Simon set up the monitors, and Linus asked him if he'd learned anything about Balfour's and Chen's deaths.

"It just came in this morning. I convinced the authorities in the U.S. to forward me a copy of the report on the crash that killed them." Oliver scooped a sheaf of papers from the printer tray. "With everything else going on I don't have time to look at it, but here you go."

"Thanks, Oliver. This may be just what we need."

Julia hurried to Linus's side, eager to look the papers over and learn what they could. She'd never for a moment believed the two men who'd died would have been foolish enough to tamper with Pendleton's design only to make it worse, and then kill themselves trying to prove they hadn't. Something had gone terribly wrong—she just wished she understood what.

Fortunately, Linus seemed to have enough familiarity with

reports that he flipped through the pages until he found what he wanted. "Cause of death," he said, then stabbed at the line with his finger.

She read the word aloud, "Accidental." That was all it said. And yet, "I don't believe it was accidental at all." She skimmed over the accompanying information, summarizing aloud. "The accident resulted in a fire, which burned the bodies. They had to use dental records for positive identification."

"Why would they change Pendleton's design so that it would *fail?*" Linus was clearly grappling with the same question that haunted her. "Were they that bad at engineering?"

Having intended to look up their credentials anyway, Julia turned to the computer in the corner of the room and opened up separate tabs, searching the men's full names individually. "They both studied at prestigious universities and held high degrees in their field. They had only worked at Seattle Electronics for a little over a year, hired to replace Pendleton who was let go for trying to sell the design. But even if they'd only worked there a short time, they ought to have known better," she informed Linus, who'd been poring over the rest of the report.

"Maybe they *did* know better." Linus narrowed his eyes as he pointed to a line among the search results. "Does this say Chen worked for Motormech?"

Julia clicked on the article and skimmed through the contents. "Not just Chen. Balfour is listed on this Motormech project, as well. This article was dated mere months before the engineers were hired by Seattle Electronics. It looks like they went straight from jobs with Motormech, to working for the competitor. But why? What prompted them to leave?"

"Were they upset with Motormech?" Linus mused.

"But then, why sabotage the competition?" Julia couldn't make sense of it. "What would they possibly have to gain?"

"It doesn't add up." Linus scowled at the accident report.

"There were only two other men on site when the test occurred. Those men were the sole witnesses."

"More engineers overseeing the results of the test?"

"No. Security personnel. Tom Klein and Hugo Roland."

Julia opened up two more tabs and searched for each of the names.

A row of images appeared along with the search results.

Linus sucked in a breath behind her, planting one hand squarely on the back of her chair while he reached toward the screen with the other. "Enlarge this image."

Julia clicked on it, and watched Hugo Roland's face fill the screen.

Planting his hands sideways in front of the screen, Linus covered all but the man's eyes and the bridge of his nose.

"What do you think—" Julia began, her heart thumping ominously.

"Can we find more pictures of this guy? Maybe a full body image?"

While Julia clicked through image search results, Linus paced behind her. The man he'd fought on the beach had been wearing a mask. Night had fallen, and most of the man's face had been in shadows.

And yet, the instant Linus had seen the picture of Hugo Roland on the screen, he'd felt as though the man he'd fought had jumped out at him.

"Linus," Julia said, her voice held a mixture of fear and triumph. "He's listed here at six-two, one-seventy-five."

"That's close enough to one-eighty. Can you find a shoe size on him?" Linus glared at the image on the screen.

"Do you think it's him?"

"I'm nearly certain. If the shoe fits…"

Julia clicked through the search results. "I don't like this guy," she muttered every time she came upon a new bit of information. "I really don't like this guy."

Linus wasn't going to say the words out loud, but he figured the duchess had every reason not to like either of the men who'd witnessed the engineers' deaths. From everything he could put together, Hugo Roland had been the man who'd attacked Julia on the beach. Tom Klein may well have been his accomplice. The two certainly had a record of working together—and a record of working for Motormech.

"We need to get these pictures out to all the border crossings, the airports, all the area authorities…" Julia suggested.

"Sure thing. But if these are the same guys who broke into the palace this morning, they're already in Lydia. They're not going anywhere near the borders until they have their hands on what they came for."

"My laptop?" Julia shrank the browser, apparently unwilling to look at the pictures of her attackers any longer. "Or the file that's on it, anyway."

"What's so important about that design?" Linus wanted to rehash what they knew in hopes of gaining some new insight. "Nothing was wrong with it when Pendleton designed it, but it was tampered with to cause a malfunction that resulted in injuries and the deaths of Balfour and Chen, who made the changes to the design in the first place."

"But why?" Julia stood and faced him.

Linus wished he knew the answer. "Roland and Klein were the only witnesses to Balfour and Chen's 'accident.' But what if the engineers weren't testing the engine at all? What if they weren't even conscious—maybe not even alive at that point? The real cause of death may have been destroyed in the fire."

Julia grabbed his arm. "You think Roland and Klein may have set up the test to cover up their murder?"

Linus nodded. "If Balfour and Chen tampered with the design so that it would malfunction, they'd know better than to test the engine themselves, or at least not to go faster than 75 mph when doing so."

"Roland and Klein may have killed them to keep them quiet about the engine alterations," Julia concluded. "The same way they murdered Fletcher to keep him from revealing the change from his original design."

"But who are Roland and Klein? And why do they care so much about this engine?"

Julia reached for the computer again, and enlarged the tab that held her search results. "My guess is they're a couple of hired hit men. Someone else is behind this—someone with enough money to buy silence, and a very strong reason for wanting the SE323 to fail."

"Motormech?" Linus whispered.

Julia met his eyes. "Motormech is a highly respected company in the Seattle area. A lot of people would consider them above suspicion."

"They're the only other name on the file." Linus turned to the burnt paper photographs he'd been spreading out on the table. "Motormech's name appears on these pages. It's about the only significant thing I've been able to pick out, other than a bunch of spotty filler words that don't make any sense."

Julia moved closer and peered down at the pages with him. "What other words did you find?"

Linus pulled out his notepad with its senseless scrawlings and read off the meaningless mess of letters. "Squigg. Envirotek. EEGS."

"Seriously?" Julia tugged the notepad closer and stared at the words herself. "Those are companies, Linus—companies Motormech bought up when they were on the brink of bankruptcy and failure, then turned them around to become highly profitable businesses. EEGS stands for Elite Engineers of Greater Seattle. Half their elite engineers died when their experimental aircraft crashed in the desert of New

Mexico. By the time their bodies were found…" Julia closed her mouth and looked at him, confusion warring on her face. She dropped her voice to a whisper. "They had to use dental records to identify them."

Linus watched Julia's face as the realization sank in. He couldn't bring himself to speak out loud, but he could guess exactly what she was thinking. Motormech had bought up the other companies after they'd failed under suspicious circumstances.

Motormech wasn't above suspicion after all.

FIFTEEN

Julia scoured the internet for everything she could learn about Squigg, Envirotek and EEGS. Sure enough, all three companies had experienced a nasty incident that had decimated their value and put them on the brink of ruin. Motormech had scooped them up for pennies on the dollar and saved the day.

Except that, as Julia was now nearly certain, Motormech hadn't saved the day at all. They'd caused the disaster that had ruined their smaller competitors, then bought out what was left for next to nothing and made an astronomical profit. And conveniently, it seemed anyone who might have blown the whistle on them met with an unfortunate accidental death.

Of course, as Julia realized when she read through Motormech's brochure, not all the companies they'd acquired over the years had come to them under duress. Some of them appeared to be legitimate acquisitions—enough to divert suspicion, she supposed. And anyway, Motormech could afford to make legitimate purchases now and then, with all the profit they were raking in from the lives they'd ruined.

The new knowledge burned inside her, and she wished she had someone to tell, but Linus had gone off to report what they'd learned to Jason, and hadn't returned.

"Miss Miller?" An unfamiliar voice spoke from the doorway.

Julia recognized Sam, who'd been appointed to guard her before.

"Your sister is asking for you. I'm to escort you to lunch?"

"Sure. Thanks." Julia tried to ignore the twinge of disappointment she felt at heading off with Sam at her side instead of Linus. Anyway, she had more important things to worry about, like getting through lunch without letting on to Monica all that was on her mind.

Her sister rose from the table and greeted her with a hug.

"I've got it!" the queen exclaimed, her eyes sparkling.

"Got what?"

"Your dress for tomorrow's ceremony. You'll need to have it fitted this afternoon. It's gold, to complement your topaz jewels."

"Jewels," Julia echoed. She hadn't realized there would be jewels involved. She hadn't even given any thought to her dress, since Monica had assured her she was taking care of it. "I thought it was just a title."

"Every titled royal needs royal jewels," Monica said as she floated back to her place at the table, still beaming. "Are you surprised? I wanted it to be a surprise, but you're always so good at figuring things out, I never can seem to surprise you."

"I *am* surprised," Julia assured her sincerely as she took her place at the table. Surprised, and a little bit humbled that her sister had been planning such a gift for her, and Julia hadn't even thought to be suspicious.

"Where are you?" Jason wanted to know. Linus thought his boss sounded impatient, and maybe even a little angry.

"I'm on my way home from church. I had my phone turned off for the service."

"What time are you planning to be here?"

"You said all hands report at one. It's not even noon yet."

"Yes, but we need to see if this tuxedo fits. You were supposed to try it on yesterday before you left."

"Tuxedo?"

"To escort the duchess." Jason sounded more than just impatient now.

"I thought I'd be wearing my dress uniform."

Jason growled something incoherent, and it occurred to Linus that the head guard was under a tremendous amount of stress trying to keep Julia and the rest of the royals safe under particularly trying circumstances.

"Just get yourself over here as fast as you can, and pray this suit fits because I don't want the royal guard to look bad."

"I'll be there as soon as I can," Linus promised, and turned off the route home, heading instead directly to the palace.

Linus straightened the bow tie and studied his reflection skeptically. The tuxedo wasn't a perfect fit—it was plenty large around the waist. They must have ordered it with extra room to accommodate his body armor, not realizing how thin the steel plates he wore really were. But the tailor had shoved sturdy safety pins into the pants so they wouldn't droop, and the jacket covered the pins, so he figured it would have to be good enough. Linus still wasn't clear on why he couldn't just wear his royal guard uniform—something about the formality of the occasion, the international image of the royal family, and looking nice for pictures.

Whatever. Jason had told him to wear the tux, and he knew how to follow orders.

"Linus." Nick trotted up to him and whispered discreetly. "Scott Gordon died this morning."

Though the news didn't surprise him, Linus nonetheless felt his heart give a mournful twist. He knew they'd done all they could for the man, but he still felt guilty they hadn't been able to save him.

"Scott's mother is here," Nick continued. "She wants to see Julia."

"Is that okay?"

"Jason cleared it. Can you take the woman to the throne room and introduce them?"

"I guess."

"Give her ten minutes, then move her out. We're on a tight schedule."

Nick was halfway out the door as he spoke, and Linus followed to find Nick speaking to a small, graying woman who clutched something that looked like a photo album. "Phyllis, this is Linus Murati. He'll take you to see Julia," Nick explained before departing quickly.

"I'm sorry for your loss," Linus said as he took the woman's hand and felt his throat swell. He didn't know what else to say.

The woman seemed to be in a daze, anyway. "Thank you." She took his arm and he led her down the familiar hallway toward the throne room.

The large hall felt cool, though the chandeliers above were all lit and the room bustled with activity. A photographer occupied the center of the room, orchestrating the placement of royals on the raised dais where King Thaddeus and Queen Monica sat upon their thrones.

Julia stood down one step near her sister, her body turned at an angle.

Though he'd expected to see her, Linus nearly stumbled at the sight of the lovely duchess, her hair all done up and topped with a tiara, her graceful figure draped in a flowing golden gown. Had he ever seen anyone so beautiful?

"Who is this?" The photographer asked as they approached.

"Phyllis Gordon," Linus explained. "She needs to talk to Julia." He looked at Julia, overcoming his awe to explain,

"Scott's mother." Suddenly he wondered if Julia had heard that Scott was dead—if she even knew his death had been pending. Last he'd told her, Scott had come out of surgery but had yet to awaken. If she didn't know, it was too late to tell her now.

"Fine, we'll take a short break," the photographer announced as Julia lifted her skirt just high enough to reveal jeweled slippers as she stepped down the last dais steps and approached Phyllis, sympathy on her face.

Phyllis held out the album. "Scott wanted me to give this to you. He had been trying to reach you for days. I think he knew…" Her voice drifted off slightly, but then she called her attention back to Julia. "I looked through these papers. I think they're the reason Scott was killed, but I don't understand any of it. Could you—" the woman's voice broke for just a moment before she regained control "—could you sort it out? I want my son's killer brought to justice."

Julia's eyes glimmered, and though Linus sensed she hadn't known of Scott's death until then, sympathy poured from her. She accepted the album and embraced the woman.

"Thank you. I think I know why those men were after Scott, and you're probably right. If he gave you these papers, they're sure to help us. We won't let his killers go free."

"That's all I can ask." Phyllis looked up at Linus. "I'm ready to go now."

Linus led the woman toward the palace entrance, where her daughter had been waiting. After offering his condolences and feeling reassured that a member of the palace staff was seeing to their needs, Linus left them and hurried back to the throne room.

Julia still stood in the same spot where he'd left her, pouring over the contents of the binder Phyllis had given her. She looked up when he reached her side. "I think these are copies of the papers that were burned. Scott must have left a copy in Seattle with his mom, before he came to Lydia to try to find me."

"I'm glad he did. I spent my afternoon on the phone with detectives from the Seattle police yesterday. They were glad to have information on Fletcher's murder, but they insisted we'd need solid evidence before they could go after Motormech."

"This binder should give them some of that evidence. I don't have time to sort through it now, but everything fits together. I'd been hoping to talk to you sooner—I looked into those other companies, and I think I see a pattern. We might have enough evidence to make a case, but we need to know who's been giving Klein and Roland their orders."

"And we'll have to catch whoever's behind it. It's not enough to just take out Klein and Roland, or the real brains behind it all will only hire more hit men."

Julia nodded solemnly. "You're right. Motormech seems determined to cover up anything that might link them to the crime. When Fletcher started asking questions, they altered my files so he couldn't get his hands on any solid proof against them."

"And when that only aroused Scott's suspicions, they felt they had to take more drastic steps."

"I don't know what Scott had to do to get his hands on all these documents, but he clearly drew enough attention to his actions that they decided to eliminate him, too."

"And that led them back to you." Linus scowled with frustration. "It's not fair that they know so much about us, and we know nothing about the real party behind all this."

Before Julia could speak, the photographer returned to the center of the room and clapped impatiently. "Let's get back to our places!"

"I should get going." Julia handed him the binder. "Can you take care of this?"

"Sure thing. Then I'll be right back."

Julia watched Linus hurry away and prayed God would watch over the evidence, as well as the man who carried it. Linus looked even more perfect than usual in his tuxedo.

Julia took the spot at her sister's arm and smiled for the camera as instructed, but on the inside, she was full of doubts and questions. Had she pushed Linus away by getting too close the morning before? He'd explained to her why he couldn't get involved with her, and she understood that. Was he keeping his distance in order to ensure they didn't cross any lines? Or was he having second thoughts about his feelings?

No matter how much she longed to learn how he felt about her, there always seemed to be other pressing matters to discuss. Until they found out who was behind everything, she doubted she'd learn how Linus really felt.

The rest of the afternoon passed in a blur of flashbulbs and pomp. Julia tried to enjoy the events, but armed guards hovered on the periphery, a constant reminder of the danger that wasn't afraid to breach the palace walls. Though she knew the ceremony would have been rescheduled if the royal advisors had thought it necessary, nonetheless, Julia couldn't shake the fear that something might happen at any moment.

The ceremony, as she might have predicted, was a moving, emotional affair. The members of the royal family proceeded in ahead of her, looking radiant in their formal wear. Princess Anastasia, the youngest sister of the current king, entered first, with her fiancé, Kirk Covington, on her arm. Julia had heard the story of how Kirk, a rogue guard, and Anastasia had survived the attacks earlier in the summer, by hiding out on one of the islands off the Lydian coast. No one seemed to know which island, though. When asked, she and Kirk simply winked at one another and smiled secretively.

Anastasia was followed by her sister, Princess Isabelle, whose adventures during the attacks had included escape via the catacombs of Charlemagne beneath the city. Her fiancé, Levi Grenaldo, escorted her in.

Next, the king's only brother, Alexander, the soldier prince, entered with his fiancée, Lillian Bardici, who'd saved his life during the attacks. Behind them, the royal parents, the former King Philip and Queen Elaine walked in slowly. Julia was surprised to see the former king walking without any assistance, save for his wife's supporting arm. Philip had nearly died after being shot defending his daughters and still used a walker to get around the palace.

Finally, the orchestra changed its tune, and trumpets blared as King Thaddeus took his place in the doorway with Queen Monica on his arm. Their son, five-year-old Peter, walked in just ahead of them, looking uncertain for just a moment before he spotted his grandparents up ahead. Then he beamed and walked confidently toward them.

Julia's throat caught as she watched her beloved nephew, his pale hair combed almost flat, his miniature tuxedo making him look like a little man. Monica shimmered under her royal jewels, but Julia couldn't shake the thought that her sister looked fragile, almost dwarfed by the richly inlaid crown atop her head.

Then it was her turn to proceed. Linus held her arm steady as they approached the thrones where her sister stood next to the king. The music ended and the crowd was seated, though Julia remained standing as the service continued with solemn readings from the ancient annals of Lydia's royal history.

After King Thaddeus settled the tiara into place on her head, Monica stepped forward. The plan had been for her to place one hand on Julia's shoulder and offer a few words of blessing, but they ended up embracing and using the formal scarlet kerchief from King Thaddeus's pocket to dry their happy tears.

The familiar notes of the Lydian national anthem filled the ballroom, and all those assembled sang the ancient song together. Julia was glad she'd taken the time to learn the words, memorizing the lyrics by singing along to a video she'd found online. The royal siblings looked pleasantly surprised to hear her singing confidently with them, and when Julia glanced at the former king and queen, Elaine winked at her.

Julia nearly faltered then and felt her throat swell with tears. But Linus held one hand over hers where she grasped his arm, and he gave her hand a slight squeeze, reassuring her.

She made it through the song, and somehow through the recessional, with everyone who'd come in ahead of her exiting before her. Through it all Linus stood at attention in his place, ready to lead her wherever she needed to go. He stood beside her in the receiving line as dignitaries from area nations shook her hand, or nodded or bowed according to their custom.

When he disappeared for a moment, she felt a surge of fear that something might have happened. She glanced at the guards along the walls, but they looked as stoic as ever. And then Linus returned to her side. "Thirsty?" He held out a full glass of punch.

"What would I do without you?" She accepted the glass gratefully.

After an informal hour of hors d'oeuvres presented by circling wait staff bearing trays, the orchestra began to play, and Monica cornered her to ask if she was ready to dance.

"Dance?" Julia felt sure she'd have remembered that part if she'd been warned ahead of time.

But Monica only laughed off her fears and pointed her in the right direction.

"Do you know how to dance?" Julia asked Linus in a whisper as he led her to the center of the floor.

"I have three older sisters," he explained with a wry smile. "They used me as a practice dummy. Just don't ask me to jitterbug. Things might get a little crazy."

His words brought a smile to her lips and eased her fears. Once she had the rhythm down and the cameras eased their most frantic snapping, she relaxed and took advantage of a moment to chat. "You've got your earpiece in," she noted. "Anything happening?"

"Everything's been quiet so far. I hope your theory was right. Klein and Roland should know better than to try to get to you at such a populated event."

"I'm grateful for that. I'd hate for anything to happen with all these people here. There'd be too great a chance of someone getting hurt. But still…" Her words drifted off as more flashbulbs snapped, distracting her.

"Still?" Linus asked after they'd circled the floor for a few smooth moments.

"I don't want to sound like I'm asking for trouble, but I almost wish something would happen while we have extra security in place. We're prepared for them, or as prepared as we've ever been. And I want so much for all of this to end. It won't end until we catch them, and I can't see how we're going to catch them if they don't make another move." She'd no sooner spoken than she apologized. "I don't want to put anyone in danger, but we're all in danger as long as the killers remain at large."

Linus heard the heartfelt note in Julia's voice. It struck a chord inside him, echoing with the same guilty resonance that had struck him when he'd realized the senseless scrawlings he'd picked out from the burnt papers were really key clues to solving the case.

"Don't apologize for wanting to see justice served," he murmured near her ear as the music changed and their steps slowed to match the rhythm.

She drifted closer to him, and he was glad to have her there, though he cautioned his heart not to leap with too much joy, because she wasn't his, not even for a moment. "If anyone needs to apologize, I do."

"Why?" Julia's surprise seemed sincere.

"I didn't recognize the names of the other companies Motormech bought out."

"I'm sure very few people outside of the Seattle area or technology fields would have recognized those names."

"But I had the brochure. I could have made the connection two days ago—"

"What do you mean by that? You picked out those names from the burnt documents, when I'd pored over them and spotted nothing but random letters. You didn't get in the way, you moved the case forward."

Linus wanted to make her understand, but he realized at her comments that he blamed himself for more than just missing the clue. She was royalty now, and he was just her guard. He couldn't act on his feelings toward her. He didn't even have a right to raise the issue.

"You're right," he rushed to apologize. "I'm sorry. I didn't mean to upset you."

Julia pulled slightly closer, her perfume swirling around him as they twirled across the floor. "I'm not upset—" Her voice broke.

Alarmed, Linus pulled back far enough to get a clear look at her eyes. "Julia," he tried to soothe her, tried to keep them dancing smoothly across the floor, but her steps faltered and he realized she was no longer up to dancing.

They'd made it through the first couple of songs, anyway. Could they slip away?

"I'm all right," she said with a sniffle, not sounding the least bit all right.

"Let's step out for some air."

Julia didn't answer out loud, only sniffled more as she leaned on his arm and he led her from the dance floor.

"Everything okay?" Simon's voice buzzed in his earpiece.

As they escaped to the relative privacy of the hallway, Linus replied. "The duchess just needs a little air. Everything okay on your end?"

"All clear here. Tell the duchess to enjoy her evening."

"Sure thing."

They reached the interior courtyard and strolled toward the gardens, where the fountain was lit with colored lights, and strands of tiny white bulbs encircled the topiaries, casting a romantic glow across the flowers and hedges.

Julia inhaled the fresh air. "It's a lovely night."

To Linus's relief, Julia sounded calmer. The tranquil garden had a soothing effect on him as well, and he breathed out the tension he'd been feeling. After all the preparations they'd made, fearing for the worst, it seemed the night was going to go off without a hitch. The sounds of the orchestra filtered out through the open palace windows, and Linus imagined the swirling couples they'd left behind on the dance floor.

Suddenly his earpiece snapped to life again. "Get the duchess to a secure location. We're locking down the ballroom."

"What's the situation?" Linus asked as he guided Julia swiftly back in the direction of the palace.

"We have visual confirmation on the west wall. Two men have breached the perimeter. They knocked out the guard who tried to intercept them."

"Where are they now?"

"It's unclear," Simon responded, his attention clearly on learning the answer to that exact question. "I have running figures in the garden, but it's too dark to say if they're friend or foe."

Linus rushed Julia toward the shallow steps to the cobbled courtyard.

"What is it?" Julia asked, holding her long gown up above her feet with one hand as she bounded up the stairs, clinging to his arm with her other hand for balance.

"Perimeter breach. They may be in the garden."

Julia glanced behind them and gasped. "It's Roland," she said, then shrank against Linus. "He has a gun!"

SIXTEEN

Julia shrank against the marble column as Linus covered her.

She didn't hear the sound of shooting, but hardly found its absence reassuring.

Linus spoke in low, urgent tones into his earpiece as he held her tight against the cold pillar. "We have one armed perp in the garden. He's north of the fountain, skirting the hedges slowly. I don't think he knows we've seen him."

Julia could only guess that the splashing water from the fountain, combined with the orchestra music still pouring out of the palace, had kept Roland from hearing Linus. And with the cover of the many blooms and hedges, perhaps the man hadn't spotted them yet.

Or perhaps he only wanted them to think he hadn't seen them.

"Let's get inside," Julia said as she clung to Linus's lapels, feeling exposed in the wide open courtyard.

"They've locked down the ballroom to keep the intruder out," Linus explained.

Julia closed her eyes, knowing it was for the best. From what she'd heard of the plans being laid in the past two days, if there was any breach of security, the palace would be locked down, but the events would continue on schedule to avoid panicking the crowd. The people dancing in the ballroom were likely oblivious to the fact that the doors had been locked all around them, and that an armed intruder was creeping along the hedges just outside.

"The executioner's escape," she whispered to Linus, who seemed focused on whatever updates he was receiving via his earpiece. "If we stay low on the stairs, the balustrade will shield us until we get inside."

She felt Linus's nose brush her ear as he spoke in an urgent whisper.

"They've got the gunman on camera. He's moving to the left." Linus changed tones, addressing his fellow guards. "Tell me the moment his back is turned, and we'll make a break for it."

Julia tensed, holding her long skirts well off her feet, poised to run the instant Linus got the signal.

The courtyard seemed deceptively peaceful. If she hadn't seen the gunman with her own eyes, she would have had trouble believing that any threat could be lurking in the verdant gardens.

"Now!" Linus darted for the stone steps, ducking low as he ran with one arm looped around Julia's waist, half shielding, half carrying her as they bounded together up the stairs, taking the shallow steps in twos and threes.

Julia couldn't see her feet, but trusted that Linus's steady grip would keep her from falling. Far more than a tumble down the stairs, she feared that the man behind them would see them in time to get a shot off in their direction.

To her relief, more columns shielded them from view as they paused at the blank wall of stones that camouflaged the secret entrance. "How did we open this last time?" she whispered, frantically searching with her fingers for the protruding stone that had served as a handle.

Linus found it first and gave it a tug just as Julia heard plinking against the columns behind them. He shoved her through the opening and followed, pulling the door closed tight behind them.

"He's got a silencer on his gun."

"Those were bullets hitting the pillar?" Julia panted hard from the combination of their sudden sprint and the surging fear she felt.

"I'm afraid so," Linus said as he wrapped his arm around her again. "He spotted us."

"Is there any way to lock that thing behind us?" Julia couldn't see anything in the pitch black of the stone chamber.

"Not that I know of." Linus fumbled with something, and a tiny penlight pierced the darkness with its slender beam. "We've got to keep moving."

Julia wanted to ask which way he thought they should go, but Linus was back to talking into his earpiece again, instructing the other guards to apprehend the man in the courtyard. Knowing how many extra soldiers they had on duty that night, Julia reassured herself that the man would be quickly apprehended, and the guests in the ballroom would never have to know about the danger just beyond the palace walls.

But Linus tensed beside her. "What? No." He spoke into the earpiece. "We have a gunman in the courtyard." He sounded upset.

"What is it?"

"The guards are caught up containing the protests of irate guests who believe they should be allowed to leave the ballroom. With a greater potential for loss of life, their immediate safety takes precedence over going after the gunman."

"No," Julia moaned, but her voice was buried under the sound of stone grating on stone.

A beam of light filtered in behind them.

"The stairs," Linus whispered as he scooped her up again, bounding up the spiraling stairs with his arm slung around her waist.

It was all Julia could do to keep her skirt free of her feet. As they came to the third floor landing, she instinctively leaned toward the panel that would take them outside.

"No," Linus cautioned her. "To the roof!"

But a bullet ricocheted through the stairwell chamber, and Linus quickly changed his mind. "All right then."

Julia realized as Linus leaned into the blank wall with his shoulder that they'd never figured out how to open the passageway. His phone had rung while they'd been exploring, and they'd never made it past that point. She didn't know what lay beyond.

The false wall gave way under the pressure of Linus's shoulder and he pushed her though the opening, pulling the wall closed after them.

"Shh." He buried his face in her hair so that he spoke directly into her ear with the softest of whispers. "He may not know which way we went."

Julia tensed, grateful for Linus's arms around her. Just beyond the pounding of her heart, she heard a slight, shuffling echo as Hugo Roland scurried up the stairs. The sound faded upward, and Julia tightened her grip on Linus's arm, praying Roland would miss them, praying the other guards would catch him before he realized where they'd gone.

"Is the third-floor courtyard balcony clear?" Linus inquired into his earpiece.

But a moment later, the scuffling sound was back, growing louder as the steps drew closer, pausing at the landing where they'd pushed through the wall. Then a soft scratching indicated the man was feeling along the wall for the way through.

Linus didn't speak, but Julia gathered the guards must have told him that the courtyard was clear, because he swept his fingers along the outer wall, searching for a latch before shoving against the stones with his shoulder.

The wall cracked open in front of them just as the partition behind them gave way.

Julia squeezed through the narrow space, hoping to pull Linus out after her, but he recoiled back into the narrow space between the doorways, and she realized with desperate fear that he was going to try to take out the gunman by himself.

"Stay clear—get down!" Linus instructed her as he dived back toward the armed man.

Linus knew he'd only have the advantage of surprise for a split second. He couldn't waste it. More than that, he couldn't allow Roland to follow them out onto the balcony. There would be nowhere to hide, no way to shield the duchess except with his own body—and if the gunman brought him down, Julia would have no protection at all.

Instead he threw himself at the false wall between them the moment the man started through the opening, leading with his gun drawn.

Crack!

The stones caught Roland in the shoulder, squeezing him between the facade and its frame, but at the same moment, he squeezed the trigger.

The shot went wild. Linus grabbed Roland by the arm and slammed his hand against the wall, trying to knock the gun from his hand. When that didn't work, he tried to pry it from his fingers.

But with both hands on the gun, Linus couldn't keep the man from squeezing into the tiny room between the two false walls. With desperate urgency, he forced the gun from Roland's hand.

It clattered against the stone floor.

The man was through the door now, and there was hardly room in the narrow space for Linus to pull back his arm, let alone swing his leg around to kick the man. Instead he tackled him, lunging atop his shoulders and trying to force him back the way he'd come. But his oversize attacker only pushed his way forward, slamming Linus against the wall.

Linus slid low, trying to punch his attacker, to push him away, but there wasn't room to maneuver. Roland slipped one arm up and got him in a headlock, tearing at his hair, his ears, and the wire to his earpiece, which he tore free and flung away, taking the microphone with it.

"Linus!" Julia gasped from the doorway.

He turned his head to shout at her, to urge her to get away, but even as he spotted the figure behind her, the man spoke.

"Freeze!"

It was Tom Klein. He swung the stone door open wide as he prodded Julia forward with the barrel of his gun.

Beyond them, in the rosy glow of the fountain's lights, Linus glimpsed his fellow guards stealthily approaching the courtyard from the garden. From what he could tell, their attackers were unaware of the guards approaching.

But they were too late. Klein shoved Julia hard against Linus, stepped in after her, and closed the false wall tight behind them. "Upstairs," he grunted, and Julia stifled a tiny gasp which could only mean he'd prodded her again with his gun. "To the roof."

Roland had taken advantage of the interruption to reclaim his gun from the floor. The moment he had the barrel pointed at them, Julia made a tiny wincing sound, and Linus angled his head around just far enough to see Klein slip a pair of handcuffs around her wrists.

Linus would have lunged toward them, but he was too far from the gun. Anything he tried now would likely only endanger Julia. A moment later, the man stepped past her, jerked Linus's arms behind his back, and cuffed him, as well.

Linus's heart sank. If he'd had any shot at overpowering the two armed men, of gaining the upper hand during a moment of distraction, his hope was lost now. Without the use of his arms or hands, any fight he might try to start would be over quickly, and then he and the duchess would be only that much worse off. There was nothing for it but to do what the men said, and to pray. The words of the twenty-fifth Psalm cycled furiously through his thoughts.

Save me from my enemies. Those who trust in You are not defeated, but those who rebel against You are defeated. Linus glanced at the two henchmen who'd brought them so much trouble over the past week. They'd likely been the ones to pull the trigger on Fletcher Pendleton and Scott Gordon as well. But even then, they weren't the real enemy. Someone else was giving them orders.

Linus wondered if he'd ever learn who the real mastermind was behind Motormech's deceits. He'd only ever seen Klein and Roland. Together the two of them ushered Linus and Julia up the stone steps toward the roof. Linus had no choice but to do what they said. He couldn't risk Julia being injured.

He could only pray his fellow guards would figure out what was happening and put a stop to it—but they'd have to be careful. If the guards burst in and spooked Klein or Roland, both he and the duchess would surely be shot.

And without his communication device, he couldn't even warn the guards to stay away.

Julia stumbled up the stairs, goaded on by the prod of the gun barrel in her back, hindered by her long gown and the slippers on her feet. At least the men had cuffed her wrists in front of her. She was able to more or less hold her skirt off her feet as she toppled up the stairs, now and again careening into Linus's side without the free use of her arms for balance.

They reached the top of the stairs. No sooner had Julia guessed they'd come to the roof than Roland tugged the hatch open and shoved her through it.

She stumbled to her feet on the gentle slope of the tiled roof. For a few fleeting seconds they stood in the open air, and Julia wondered what the men's intentions were. Then a helicopter appeared out of the night sky and touched down on a flat stretch of roof along the peak.

The gunmen pushed them toward the craft, its blades still spinning.

"Don't get on the helicopter," Linus whispered as he flung himself backward against the gunmen.

Startled, Julia ducked. She understood why Linus didn't want her aboard the chopper—she feared that if they got on, they'd never return to the palace. Not alive, anyway.

She spun around in time to see Linus take out one of the men with a leaping kick. He landed on his feet, but between the slope of the roof and his inability to use his bound hands for balance, it took him a moment to recover. In that time, the other figure advanced and clapped him across the cheek with his gun.

"Get on board!" the man shouted, shoving Linus at Julia while brandishing his gun.

Julia had no choice but to go where she was pushed. It was difficult enough to keep her balance and not slip down the tiles while going the direction they shoved her. Though she couldn't fault Linus for his courage, his skirmish had angered the gunmen. They looked ready to shoot if provoked any further.

They shoved Linus ahead of her into the copter, kicking him in the legs as they pushed him in. Then one of the gunmen plucked her up by her arms and tossed her inside. Before she had her bearings the door was closed, and she felt her stomach dip as the craft lifted off again.

Julia struggled to catch her breath and assess her position. The helicopter didn't have any seats, just a carpeted floor where she and Linus had been flung against the far wall. She felt the rise and fall of Linus's shoulder with each breath and realized she'd landed with her face pressed against him, her tiara knocked askew, her knee throbbing from being knocked against the doorway of the helicopter when they'd tossed her in.

"Are you all right?" she asked Linus in a whisper, praying he'd say he was.

"Shut up!" one of their captors shouted from behind her.

She startled at the sound and clamped her mouth shut, wondering where they were taking her and how she was ever going to get away.

They couldn't have gone far, because moments later the helicopter sank down and the blades ceased their furious churning. Bright lights assaulted her eyes as Roland and Klein shoved her out onto a graveled driveway. As her eyes adjusted to the floodlights trained upon them, Julia made a number of realizations all at once.

They were above the city among the bluffs that overlooked Seaview Drive, which wound its scenic path along the cliffs overlooking the sea. She could hear the distant waves crashing as the helicopter blades stilled completely.

But closer still and of greater concern, Julia saw more men approaching. They strode past a vehicle that gleamed in the floodlights.

Julia blinked.

It was the SE323. She'd studied enough production sketches and product brochures to recognize the thing and to feel a nauseous surge of fear at the sight of the car which became a death trap once the speedometer hit 75 miles per hour.

It was surely no coincidence that the men who'd been trying to capture her had brought her here, to this vehicle. Given the circumstances surrounding Balfour's and Chen's deaths, Julia guessed what the men intended to do.

One of the approaching men laughed, and she turned to

the sound, recognizing yet another image from the brochures she'd studied.

Todd Martin, the Motormech CEO. "I see you recognize this vehicle. Good." His laughter froze with the iciness of his words. "Then you will understand the implications of all I am about to say. I have, as you are no doubt aware, a very successful business. Thousands of people depend on me for jobs, for designs that make their lives more efficient. I am a hero."

Everything inside Julia rebelled against the thought. Those jobs only existed because Motormech had destroyed the companies that had originally created them. All of Todd Martin's accomplishments had been achieved by stealing the work of others, and killing to cover up what he'd done.

The CEO continued, "I have a reputation to protect and a company to defend. You know too much, so you must be eliminated."

"You can't clear your name by killing me," Julia spat back, refusing to believe that this man who'd destroyed so many dreams could defeat her, as well. "I've already passed on some of the evidence I've gathered. Even without my explanations, too many people know what you've done. You can't kill them all."

But the blue-eyed multimillionaire only stepped closer and bent his face down toward hers, shouting louder than was necessary at such close range. "This evidence you have passed along doesn't point to *me*. It points to a fool. All the investigators need is a name to fill in the blanks. I gave them Pendleton's name, but he wanted too much to clear it, so he had to die. I tried to make your lawyer friend my scapegoat, but you wouldn't allow that, either."

Martin's blue eyes narrowed icily. "This could have been quite simple. I could have killed you and pointed all signs of guilt toward your tombstone. It would have been a clean break. Your loved ones could have turned their backs on the scandal of your involvement and gone on with their lives unscathed, but you wouldn't let them. You had to share your suspicions, didn't you? You had to get other people involved. Now your death will not be so simple."

With a snap of his leather-gloved fingers, Martin directed his men. Klein and Roland got hold of Julia, while the other men who'd approached with Todd Martin stepped forward and muscled Linus toward the SE323. They shoved her into the driver's seat and slammed the door.

"Here's the solution," the CEO continued, pulling out a thin sheaf of papers from the attaché he carried, and leaning in the open window to speak to her. "This is your suicide note, a confession of all you've done to sabotage the SE323 designs. You see, ever since you handled the initial case between Seattle Electronics and Motormech, you saw the potential for profit. By burying Seattle Electronics in scandal and debt, you hoped to force them to sell their entire company to Motormech, buying up stock on the knowledge that once Motormech fixed the design flaw, the SE323 would quickly become one of the most profitable automobiles in America. You had Pendleton and Gordon killed when they tried to expose you. *You* were behind it all."

Julia heard the man's lies and realized with horror that anyone desperate for an explanation would believe them. No one wanted to think Motormech was capable of any wrongdoing. They'd be glad to pin the blame on her. And the evidence she'd passed on would only reinforce their claims.

"My men here have tried to stop you. That's why you were attacked on the beach," Todd Martin continued his lie-filled revision of her recent history. "They tried to reach Pendleton and Gordon in time to learn the truth, but you killed them before they could speak out against you. Once you realized you could no longer cover up the truth, you confessed everything before trying to run away with your bodyguard, only to die from the very malfunction you engineered."

Julia listened in horror, trying to spot the hole in the man's plan.

But there was no hole—none he couldn't plug up with smooth words once she was dead and unable to defend herself. Everyone wanted to believe Motormech was an honest company. They wanted to see Todd Martin as a hero. They'd only be too eager to believe him and to blame every evil deed on her.

Still, she fought against his words. "No one will ever believe you," she insisted, wishing the words were really true. "They won't honestly think I wrote that note."

Todd Martin only laughed. "They will when you sign it."

"I won't sign it! You can't make me."

"You *will* sign it," Todd Martin explained, "or we'll place an anonymous call to the palace alerting them that you're here and you need help. When your precious guards and family members come rushing to your aid, they'll arrive just in time for the SE323 to crush them as it malfunctions. And so, anyone who might question why your suicide note wasn't signed, will be killed by the same accident that kills you."

Julia could only stare at him, certain his plan couldn't work, but unable to articulate a single protest against it. She didn't want to believe it possible, but what if he was right? What if Linus's fellow guards and even her concerned sister drove up the perilous roads to try to rescue her?

What if they died because of her? Even if the car didn't malfunction precisely as her concerned sister arrived, Todd Martin could have her killed and make it look as though it had.

Julia turned to Linus, hoping he'd spotted some hole in the man's plan, some way out of the predicament they were in.

His brown eyes glinted with determination. "I believe, Your Grace, you'd better sign whatever they ask you to sign."

Julia looked back at the power-hungry CEO and the gunmen who surrounded him. Todd Martin held out the papers and a pen.

"Okay," she whispered, hardly believing she was agreeing to his demands. But what else could she do? She couldn't risk letting anything happen to her sister. "I'll sign."

SEVENTEEN

Linus kept his eyes riveted on Julia while his hands worked feverishly behind him. Fortunately Todd Martin and his men seemed far more interested in Julia than in whatever Linus was doing with his fingers under the cover of his draping tuxedo jacket.

They didn't seem to realize that he'd pulled a safety pin from his pants, or that he'd already used its slender prong to unlatch the lock on the handcuffs that bound him. He'd realized in the process that the handcuffs weren't made of metal, but a strong plastic that would no doubt melt in the flames of their accident, erasing all evidence that he and the duchess had been held against their will.

But Linus got the cuffs slipped off without Martin or his men noticing. Now if he could just keep them from figuring it out long enough to get Julia safely away, and maybe even contact the rest of the guard in time to apprehend the Motormech conspirators before they left Lydia. If Todd Martin crossed the border, he'd be out of Lydian jurisdiction, and it would become vastly more difficult to capture him.

But Linus couldn't let himself be distracted by that fear. Far more pressing was the urgency of saving the duchess. With Julia's signature on the document, the only way she could prove her innocence was if she survived. If anything went wrong, Martin would get away with his evil plan.

"Thank you, duchess. Have a lovely ride." The CEO yanked her door open, shoved the running car into gear, clamped down the accelerator, and threw the door shut again as the vehicle took off down the driveway. "Try to steer, duchess!" he called after them. "We'd hate for anyone to think you died because you couldn't drive!"

Linus flew into action the moment the door was shut, throwing himself across Julia's seat and reaching for the accelerator.

It was stuck!

He pried at it, but he couldn't get it loose. What had they used to clamp it down?

It didn't matter. Having stared long enough at the SE323 design drawings, Linus knew where to find the emergency brake. He got hold of it with one hand just as he slipped his left foot past the duchess, stomping the regular brake against the floor as he pulled with all his might on the handle of the emergency brake.

White smoke poured up through the open windows against the unrelenting power of the full-throttle engine.

The combination of brakes was enough to slow the vehicle against the floored accelerator, but not enough to stop it entirely. Given how much smoke poured through the windows, Linus knew the brakes wouldn't last much longer before they were burned completely through and there was no longer any way to slow the car. And from their height on the bluffs, all roads led downhill to the rocks that edged the sea.

There was no other option. He had to get the duchess out of the car now—while it was still moving slowly enough for them to escape alive.

Unwilling to take his hands from the brake for even the slightest second, Linus asked Julia, "Can you open the door?"

With her hands still cuffed together in front of her, the duchess fumbled momentarily before successfully lifting the handle.

She was just in time. The brakes stuttered and caught, slipping repeatedly. They had to be nearly worn through. Just up ahead, Linus spotted an open field between two rocky plots of woods. If he could steer the car into the field, it would give them the best opportunity for a safe landing.

"When I say go, we're going out the door. Can you do that?"

"I'm ready."

Steering them into the open field, Linus was relieved to discover that the thick meadow grasses caught up around the tires, slowing the car's advance to barely a crawl. "Now!" Linus let go of the brake and leaped after Julia through the door, rolling free of the car as it rumbled on toward the woods, accelerating again without his pressure on the brakes.

Linus wrapped his arms around Julia as they rolled to a stop, then swept the hair from her face as he examined her for any sign of injury. "Are you all right?"

"I'm alive," she panted, looking around as though assessing the damage. Then her gaze came to rest on his face. "Because of you."

She leaned forward and Linus thought she was going to try to sit up, but instead her lips found his with an urgent kiss.

He didn't intend to kiss her back, but there was no stopping it. Relief and affection filled him as he returned her kiss.

But the sound of the SE323 crashing into the trees reminded him of all that was still at stake. He broke off their kiss and pulled out his phone. "We need to get the guard after Martin."

"You're right." Julia held tight to his arm with her cuffed hands while he dialed.

After a brief conversation, he updated Julia on what he'd

learned. "The guards are already apprehending Martin and his men. They took off in guard helicopters when they saw Martin's copter lift off the palace roof. They arrived just as the SE323 drove off, but they didn't realize we were inside it until after they were on the ground." Linus put the phone back into his pocket and pulled out another safety pin. Using the pointy tip, he quickly freed the duchess.

"Thank you." She reached for his face and kissed him again.

Linus lost track of time for a moment, thrilled by her touch and the realization that now that Todd Martin and his henchmen were caught, she didn't have to be afraid anymore. But that awareness brought another change. "Julia?" He caressed her face lovingly as she leaned against him in the meadow.

"Yes?"

"Now that you're safe—" he brushed another kiss against her cheek "—will you be going back to America?"

Julia pulled back just far enough to look into his eyes. In the evening light he couldn't read what he saw there, and she gave him no reassurances.

Instead, bright lights streamed down from above, and they both looked up to see a royal guard helicopter with Sam leaning out the door.

"There they are!" The guard pointed joyfully, then shouted down at them. "I've told the car where to find you. They'll pick you up in just a moment!"

Linus helped Julia to her feet, as she smoothed down her dress and straightened her tiara. A car he recognized from the royal garage rolled to a stop alongside the meadow a moment later. "Get in," Paul said as he pushed a door open for them. "Let's get you home."

The next day, Julia felt sore from the tumble out of the SE323. But the royal guard had apprehended Martin and his men, along with the dented SE323 and enough evidence to link them to kidnapping, attempted murder and conspiracy charges, along with Scott Gordon's murder and several other crimes they'd committed in Lydia in the process.

That in itself was a relief. More so was her sister Monica's announcement over breakfast with all their extended family present.

"We wanted to keep it a secret until after your titling ceremony. It needed to be your special day, and we knew our announcement would only cause distractions. But at the same time, all our trips to the doctor couldn't go unnoticed much longer. Nor could the toll on my health."

Julia stared at her big sister, fearing that Monica must have an awful disease. But the queen beamed as King Thaddeus took her hand in his, smiling broadly and gazing at her with adoration.

"We're pregnant," Monica explained.

And just as quickly, Thaddeus added, "with twins."

"That's why you look so awful!" Sheila Miller responded with a gasp, then blushed as she scrambled from her chair to embrace her daughter. "Oh, Monica, I'm so delighted!"

"The twins haven't made life easy," Monica admitted as she opened her arms to her mother, "and I'm not as young as I was when I had Peter."

Julia rushed to hug her sister, as well. "I'm so relieved," she whispered through her happy tears, "and so thrilled for you."

"Does this mean you'll stay?" Monica asked, looking at her intently.

"What?" Julia blinked at the queen, then looked around at all the royal family, who seemed to be anxiously awaiting her answer. "What do you mean?"

"I know you have a successful law practice in Seattle, and I hate to ask you to walk away from that, but I'm sure you'd have no trouble practicing law in Lydia if you wanted to, and it would make me so happy if you were closer, especially with the babies on the way. But I won't ask you to—"

Julia cut off her words with a big hug. "Of course I'll stay. I'd love to!"

Thaddeus's sisters and brother and their fiancés all pressed forward for a turn congratulating the couple, and Julia backed toward the door, still stunned at the news, and feeling suddenly rather alone and left out. She'd always pictured her kids and Monica's kids growing up together, but Monica was soon to be a mother of three, and Julia wasn't even attached to anyone. Though she was thrilled for her sister, she couldn't completely repress the feeling that she was being left behind.

She backed toward the doorway to the hall, ready to make her escape if her emotions overwhelmed her.

"I see that look." A bass voice whispered near her ear as familiar fingers slipped around her hand. "You're thinking of sneaking out again," Linus teased. "Not without a guard."

"Linus." Julia turned to him and grinned, having thought about him all morning, but not having seen him. "Did you hear the news?"

"Yes. Twins. The entire kingdom will be overjoyed."

"That, too," Julia said as she beamed at him, unsure if he'd been informed of the king's decision, which Monica had whispered to her just before breakfast. "And they're going to award you with a medal for meritorious service. I get to pin it on you in a formal ceremony with your grandfather and anyone else you want invited."

The teasing smile disappeared from Linus's face.

"Aren't you happy?"

"I am, but—" he shook his head "—they can't award me a medal without reviewing my record. Jason will have to share with them—"

"He already did."

"What?"

Julia looked up at him, brimming with emotion. "Jason shared everything on your record. They still agreed unanimously to give you a medal."

"So I get to stay on as a guard? I never thought—"

"Linus," she said as they backed into the hallway, unnoticed by the happy throng behind them, "they asked me this morning if I wanted you assigned as my primary guard."

"What did you say?"

"I asked if it mattered that I was in love with you."

"Julia." His fingers swept the side of her face affectionately. "You must know how I feel about you. I fall in love with you more and more every time we're together. If I wasn't afraid of overstepping my bounds—" he glanced toward the happy royals hugging in the room beyond them "—I might have an announcement of my own to make."

"An announcement?" Her heart skipped a beat.

"I love you, Your Grace. With all this talk of royal weddings—" he looked down at her, his eyes aglow with emotion "—I suppose it's presumptuous of me to want to claim you as my own, but you must know, I'd marry you in a heartbeat. If only it were possible."

Julia felt her mouth drop open slightly. "If you asked me, I'd say yes."

Linus grinned and cast another look toward the oblivious party in the room beyond them.

"But your family…"

"My sister would wholeheartedly approve, and the king just wants to make her happy."

"Well, in that case, would you marry me?"

"Yes." She giggled, perhaps a little too loudly. Linus silenced her happy laughter with a kiss.

"But Julia—" he kissed the tip of her nose "—we should keep this between us for a bit. There have been plenty of royal announcements lately."

"I agree. We should let them get used to the idea," she kissed him again before continuing, "After all, they might argue that we don't know each other well enough."

"I know that I love you. That's enough for me."

"I feel the same way." She cleared her throat and tried to remember the important thing she'd been going to say before he'd distracted her by proposing marriage. "Which is why I shared my feelings for you with my sister."

Linus bent his head nearer hers, his lips tauntingly close. "What did she say?"

"She's quite in favor of it as long as it doesn't get in the way of you protecting me."

Linus leaned down and kissed her then, wrapping his arms protectively around her as he drew her close. "I won't let anything get in the way of protecting you."

And he sealed his promise with another kiss.

* * * * *

Dear Reader,

The royal guards of Lydia are more than bodyguards, more than watchmen or security personnel, more than men in a symbolic uniform, marching back and forth in front of the palace gates. The men of Lydia's royal guard pledge to do all they can, by God's power, to protect the members of the royal house of Lydia.

I'm so thrilled that you've picked up this first book in the Protecting the Crown series from Love Inspired Suspense. *Defending the Duchess* is just the first book in this series. There are more tales of romance and suspense yet to come. You can check my website at www.rachellemccalla.com for updates on the latest in forthcoming titles.

As you may have guessed, Lydia is a land full of love and adventure, both in a contemporary setting, and throughout history. The Protecting the Crown series picks up where the Reclaiming the Crown series left off. Look for her next book in the series *Royal Heart* in July 2013. The Protecting the Crown series also includes Love Inspired Historical stories. *A Royal Marriage,* which was released in December of 2012, tells about King John of Lydia and Gisela, the daughter of Charlemagne. And in November 2013, look for the story of John's brother Luke.

The Christian kingdom of Lydia is a lovely place to visit at any time of year. I'm so glad you could join Linus and Julia on their adventures, and I hope you'll be back soon.

God's blessings on your journey,
Rachelle

Questions for Discussion

1. Julia travels to Lydia in large part because she is worried about her sister Monica's stress levels, and she wants to support her as she adjusts to being queen. What do you think of Julia's plan? What problems arise when we tie our goals to another person's emotional state? What complications did Julia face?

2. From an early point in the story, Linus feels attraction toward Julia. How does he deal with his growing feelings? Do you think he made the right choices? Do you respect him more or less as the story goes on?

3. As the attacks against Julia's person and property pile up, she thanks God for sending Linus to help her sort through everything. What does this tell you about her attitude and her faith? Do you think it's important to thank God for the good things, even when you're overwhelmed by bad things?

4. Linus joined the royal guard in part because of his grandfather's stories about being a royal guard. His grandfather helped him through his turbulent teenage years and kept him on the right track. Do you have people in your life who inspire and encourage you? What do you do to try to inspire and encourage others?

5. When Linus suggests to Julia that the people she works with might be connected to the attacks against her, she feels doubly distressed. Have you ever felt betrayed by a friend or associate? What is it about knowing the

perpetrator that makes a crime more awful than if a stranger committed it?

6. In spite of her feelings of betrayal, Julia still feels guilty implicating her coworkers in the case when she hands over her evidence to the police. Have you ever felt guilty for "telling on" someone? Why does Julia feel the way she does? What do you think of her choice? Have you ever been in a similar situation? How did you deal with it?

7. As the threats against them grow more serious, Julia and Linus take comfort in the words of Psalm 25. Are there any particular Psalms that bring you comfort? What is it about them that's comforting?

8. Galen let Julia exit the palace gates without a guard. Linus later notes that he'd have put Galen on leave for breach of protocol, though the sentinel had saved the lives of Princess Anastasia and Kirk two months before by defying orders from the former, corrupt head of the royal guard. What do you think of Galen's choices? Do you think Jason was right to keep him on as part of the guard in spite of his previous failures to follow the rules?

9. Julia carries a weight of guilt that her sister, Monica, has been through so many trials. Julia wishes she could have supported her more in the past, and vows to make up for that in the future. Have you ever felt guilty when someone you love suffers? What can Julia reasonably do to support her sister? What can you do to be there for those you love, and what guilty feelings do you need to let go of?

10. Linus notices how Julia likes her coffee, remembers her favorite flavored water and thoughtfully brings her a drink when she's thirsty. How do these little details communicate his feelings for her? Do you have people in your life who notice and remember things about you?

11. Scott claims he's being set up as a scapegoat. The word *scapegoat* originates in the Bible, in the Old Testament (see Leviticus chapter 16 for the full story). The scapegoat carries away the guilt so that others will no longer be guilty. In much the same way, Jesus carries the guilt of our sins so that we can live freely. How do you feel about this burden that Jesus took on for our sakes? Do you live in gratitude for the freedom he bought for you?

12. When Linus realizes that Julia might share the growing feelings he has for her, he realizes he has to confess his juvenile record. Why does Linus feel it's so important that Julia know the truth about him? How do you feel about the decision to keep him on as a guard? Where do you draw the line between justice and forgiveness?

13. Todd Martin has a glowing reputation, and his company is held in high esteem. At one point, Julia stated that she didn't want the case to cast a negative light on Todd Martin's company. Have you ever been so blinded by your regard for a person's worldly reputation that you failed to see their true motives and actions? In what ways are reputations helpful, and how can they also be problematic?

14. When Julia learns her sister's exciting news, she quickly makes up her mind to leave her old life behind and move to Lydia. What do you think of her decision? What other factors may have prompted her to make this choice?

15. Linus and Julia want to marry, but they've decided not to announce anything until they've gotten to know each other better. Do you think they make a good match? Are you happy that Julia has chosen to stay in Lydia? What would you do in her situation?

COMING NEXT MONTH
from Love Inspired® Suspense
AVAILABLE APRIL 2, 2013

EXPLOSIVE SECRETS
Texas K-9 Unit
Valerie Hansen
Alone, pregnant and terrified, Nicki Johnson has been implicated in a crime. Can police officer Jackson Worth and his K-9 partner prove her innocence and keep her safe?

PRIME SUSPECT
Falsely Accused
Virginia Smith
She'd been in the wrong place at the wrong time—and now Darcie Wiley was framed for murder. She must depend on private investigator Caleb Buchanan to clear her name, but someone will do anything to ensure Darcie's secrets stay buried.

UNDERCOVER COWBOY
Laura Scott
FBI agent Logan Quail can't turn away from a woman in danger. So when Kate Townsend is targeted by the mob, he risks his cover, his badge—and his life—to keep her safe.

HIDDEN IN PLAIN VIEW
Diane Burke
After surviving a shooting that has stolen her memories, Sarah Lapp suddenly finds herself in the protection of Samuel King, the undercover cop sent to guard her and her Amish community.

LISCNM0313

REQUEST YOUR FREE BOOKS!

2 FREE RIVETING INSPIRATIONAL NOVELS
PLUS 2 FREE MYSTERY GIFTS

Love Inspired®
SUSPENSE

YES! Please send me 2 FREE Love Inspired® Suspense novels and my 2 FREE mystery gifts (gifts are worth about $10). After receiving them, if I don't wish to receive any more books, I can return the shipping statement marked "cancel." If I don't cancel, I will receive 4 brand-new novels every month and be billed just $4.49 per book in the U.S. or $4.99 per book in Canada. That's a savings of at least 22% off the cover price. It's quite a bargain! Shipping and handling is just 50¢ per book in the U.S. and 75¢ per book in Canada.* I understand that accepting the 2 free books and gifts places me under no obligation to buy anything. I can always return a shipment and cancel at any time. Even if I never buy another book, the two free books and gifts are mine to keep forever.

123/323 IDN FVWV

Name	(PLEASE PRINT)	
Address		Apt. #
City	State/Prov.	Zip/Postal Code

Signature (if under 18, a parent or guardian must sign)

Mail to the **Harlequin® Reader Service:**
IN U.S.A.: P.O. Box 1867, Buffalo, NY 14240-1867
IN CANADA: P.O. Box 609, Fort Erie, Ontario L2A 5X3

**Are you a subscriber to Love Inspired Suspense
and want to receive the larger-print edition?
Call 1-800-873-8635 or visit www.ReaderService.com.**

* Terms and prices subject to change without notice. Prices do not include applicable taxes. Sales tax applicable in N.Y. Canadian residents will be charged applicable taxes. Offer not valid in Quebec. This offer is limited to one order per household. Not valid for current subscribers to Love Inspired Suspense books. All orders subject to credit approval. Credit or debit balances in a customer's account(s) may be offset by any other outstanding balance owed by or to the customer. Please allow 4 to 6 weeks for delivery. Offer available while quantities last.

Your Privacy—The Harlequin® Reader Service is committed to protecting your privacy. Our Privacy Policy is available online at www.ReaderService.com or upon request from the Harlequin Reader Service.
We make a portion of our mailing list available to reputable third parties that offer products we believe may interest you. If you prefer that we not exchange your name with third parties, or if you wish to clarify or modify your communication preferences, please visit us at www.ReaderService.com/consumerschoice or write to us at Harlequin Reader Service Preference Service, P.O. Box 9062, Buffalo, NY 14269. Include your complete name and address.

SPECIAL EXCERPT FROM

Love Inspired.
SUSPENSE

Nicolette Johnson is pregnant and on a crime syndicate's hit list.

Read on for a preview of the next book in the exciting TEXAS K-9 UNIT *series, EXPLOSIVE SECRETS by Valerie Hansen.*

Nicolette Johnson was about to leave for her night shift job as a short-order cook at the Highway Twenty Truck Stop when her cell phone rang.

She slipped it out of her jeans pocket and hesitated while she listened to it playing "The Yellow Rose of Texas." Most of her recent callers had been nosy reporters or curious neighbors wanting to ask what she knew about her cousin Arianna Munson's recent murder.

"That would be *nothing,* just like I told the police," she muttered. Still, she gave in and answered. "Hello?"

"Hello, Nicki, darlin'."

The slow, deep drawl was dripping with menace, sending chills up her spine. "Who is this?"

"Never mind who I am. You need to stop holding out on us," the man warned. "Remember, we know where you live."

Nicki swallowed past the lump in her throat. "I don't know what you're talking about. Leave me alone."

"That's not going to happen, lady. That idiot Murke blew it the other night, but we can still get to you, just like we got to your cousin. We eliminated her and we can do the same to you. If you think you can run or hide, just ask the Sagebrush cops what happened to one of their wives a few years back." He chortled again then shouted, *"Boom!"*

Nicki immediately ended the call. Many of the specifics of the man's threats had already become a confusing muddle but one fact stood out. The way he had barked "boom" left no doubt that she was dealing with a deadly enemy.

Shaking, Nicki managed to punch in the phone number from the business card the police officers had left with her a few days earlier. She held her breath and counted the number of rings while she waited for them to answer.

"Sagebrush Police and Sheriff. How may I help you?" a friendly sounding woman asked.

Nicki had intended to report the scary warning calmly and with little emotion. When she heard the dispatcher's voice, however, she blurted, "I need help. Somebody just threatened to blow me up!"

*Can K-9 officer Jackson Worth and his
bomb-sniffing dog, Titan, keep Nicki safe?
Pick up EXPLOSIVE SECRETS by Valerie Hansen,
available April 2013 from Love Inspired Suspense.*

SUSPENSE
RIVETING INSPIRATIONAL ROMANCE

A mafia boss wants Kate Townsend to stop asking questions...

His tactic? Send one of his thugs to intimidate her at gunpoint. FBI Agent Logan Quail knows too well what violence Bernardo Salvatore is capable of, and he doesn't hesitate to intervene...blowing his cover in the process. He wasn't able to save his fiancé. But this time, he'll make darn sure this foolhardy little filly doesn't get herself killed trying to prove her father was murdered. Now, Logan and Kate must work together, each overcoming their separate grief, to bring down a ruthless syndicate. And maybe, just maybe, find some peace through the healing power of love.

UNDERCOVER COWBOY
by
LAURA SCOTT

www.LoveInspiredBooks.com

LIS44534